Too Late For Tears

Driving rebelliously homeward, beautiful, callous Jane Palmer told her ex-Navy flier husband, attractive, mild Alan, now clerking in a small bank, that she was leaving him. Fearing he would wreck the car, she reached for the ignition key, but turned off the headlights. This apparently was a signal; a bag holding a large sum of money was thrown into their car from another car which passed them. Jane decided they would keep the money, and she would stay with Alan. Alan, however, at first wanted to call the police; he weakened the next day and decided to hold the money for a time. He checked the bag at the Union Station, said a few words, which Jane could not hear, to the attendant, and put the check in his topcoat pocket, from which it dropped into the lining. They breakfasted with Alan's pleasant sister, Katherine, who noticed that a mysterious constraint had come between them. Later, Alan grew fearful gain; he insisted that the bag be sent to the police with a note, and Jane was filled with fury.

Too Late For Tears

Roy Huggins

A MYSTERY HOUSE BOOK

TOO LATE FOR TEARS

For more titles in the Mystery House library,
visit our website: **www.FictionHousePress.com**

"Too Late For Tears", *The Saturday Evening Post*, April 4, 1947 through May 24, 1947.

isbn 978-1-64720-583-6

First Mystery House edition June 2022

Published by Fiction House Press LLC

TOO LATE FOR TEARS

As the car raced by in the darkness, someone flung out a battered handbag . . . a bag containing a fortune in cash that was destined to entangle a dozen lives in cunning intrigue, blackmail, murder. Beginning the gripping serial of a beautiful girl's ruthless pursuit of her ambition.

IT was like almost any Southern California night, a frost-bitten moon high and withdrawn among a few reluctant stars, a cool salt breeze blowing in from the sea and sweetening through the odor of brush fires in the hills.

The open convertible rolled to a slow stop before the house and the man stepped out and closed the door. The woman sat, not moving, staring out across the endless horizontal monotony of the valley. He leaned over and asked if she had gone to sleep, the tone carrying a suggestion of banter, timidly, as if he were uncertain of its reception.

The woman opened the door slowly and stepped out and stood looking at the house. She was very young, her mouth dark and full and somehow hard, and the hardness seemed to be directed at the house. It was a small house, a miniature colonial with little green shutters that were nailed down and had no hinges. Light shone behind the many-paned windows, showing stiff white curtains and the empty corner of a room. But the woman knew what was inside the house—sepia walls, and the infinite combinations of the cards, and Bill and Betty, who seemed to be two people, but were really one, a person known as Bill-and-Betty. Last night there had been a visit to Joe-and-Helen, and the night before— She shuddered, realizing that they thought of her as Alan-and-Jane. And quite suddenly the formless malady of the months past became focused and articulate.

"I can't go in there, Alan."

"Why? What's the matter, Janie?"

"Nothing!" She turned and stepped back into the car. "Hurry, they might have heard us. They might come out."

Alan had come around to the lawn that sloped down to the curb. He stepped over to her and whispered, "But if we're not going in, I've got to explain. They're expecting us, sweet. What's wrong? Are you sick?"

The breeze was suddenly cold on her forehead. "Please! Get in! You can call them later."

He waited there for a long moment, then moved abruptly and walked around and slid under the wheel. The motor turned quietly and the car lurched and moved swiftly away. She felt the tensions go. The car always did that for her. It was big and new and expensive. The night was warm and Alan was being competent at the wheel. And silent. She sat and let the night flow by, leaving the subtle odor of cottonwood in its wake, blowing gently at her soft blond hair that was like autumn floss.

They were leaving Burbank, moving up Dark Canyon toward the pass that would take them to Hollywood. Jane knew it was the car, the traffic moving by, anonymous and self-contained, Alan's silence, that made it possible for her to lie back and look at the starred sky and not think about the inescapable quarrel that must come and the things that must be said; things that had been slowly gathering for a long while. She knew they would be final and irrevocable things. A star fell in a breathless flight and broke and was gone. She smiled.

The car crossed the bridge at the pass, swung left and shot up the dark road that wound upward into the hills. Jane sat up abruptly and looked back. The way home was dropping away below.

Alan said quietly, "I asked Kathy to come in and have coffee with us when we got home. We've got to talk this out before we get there."

She turned slowly and brought up a slender leg and tucked it under her. There was a tightness in her throat that was like the beginning of exhilaration, but she waited silently.

"It isn't just tonight," he said gently. "It's been obvious for a long time. You just don't like my friends, and they know it. And there's no reason for it, Jane. They've all got a lot more than we have, and they're all nice people."

She stared past him, dimly aware of the great flat city stretching endlessly into the misty dark below. She said slowly, "You look at things as if you were seeing them through a diminishing glass. You're simple, Alan, and you think the world is simple. But it isn't. And neither am I." She had begun quietly enough, but now her throat was tight, her voice shrill. "Neither am I!"

Alan looked down at her and almost smiled. His tone changed. "Are you using that word 'simple' the way we used it in the Army, hon, or are you going literary on me?"

The gentle banter, the effort to laugh it off, jabbed sharply at her, and she flushed. Her mouth moved stiffly when she spoke. "We're through, Alan. I'm not just talking. I'm going to leave you."

The car slowed abruptly and the motor coughed. He shifted gears slowly and deliberately and the car picked up speed and rolled on. After a while he said, "Let's not go off the deep end with that kind of talk, Janie. I think we'd better skip this until tomorrow."

"I've intended to leave you all along," she said evenly. It wasn't true, but she wanted to say it just that way, with a sting in it. She saw him wince almost imperceptibly and the sense of exhilaration was strong again.

"Janie, you're getting all worked up over nothing. It's my fault. Let's drop it for now."

"There's nothing to drop, Alan. It's all been said. Perhaps I didn't really know about it until tonight . . . or even just now. But I've been cheating both of us, telling myself I'd made a go of it, grown used to it."

"Used to it? Used to what?"

"Burbank!" she cried. "And the petty, stifling life we live! I'm not like your friends. I can't delude myself that I'm happy. And I can't live on—on flummery."

He was staring stiffly out into the path of light, trying to make it out, thinking it over carefully, painfully. "I don't get it, Janie. What are you talking about?"

Jane could feel the words within her, rolling

and spilling, promising an eloquence that would crush his smug little world. But the words did not form on her lips, and there was nothing but a bitter weight inside her to show for them. She asked herself why it mattered. What was she trying to prove? She lay back against the cool leather and felt the strength of the car beneath her and was comforted by it.

After a while Alan said slowly, "I think I get the sketch, Jane. I've thought about it before in my simple way. You want to be one of the gay people. You're allergic to ruts; a home and a job and kids being the standard Number One rut." His voice was gray.

Jane didn't say anything.

"But how does one get into the mad whirl if one doesn't happen to own a couple of rubber plantations?"

It was a long time before Jane answered. "I think I know," she said distantly. "A long time ago I had that all planned. It was a daydream, of course. But I worked at it. And I think I could have brought it off." She was almost whispering now. "I suppose the 'mad whirl' is as good a word as any for what I had in mind, and I was going to marry it."

"But you married me."

"Yes."

"Of course I was a flier then; a glamour boy with ribbons and everything."

"No, Alan. Part of it was that you had the courage to live—I wish I could say 'dangerously' without sounding inane."

"I'm afraid you couldn't. Are you sure the other part wasn't that I was being shipped out? I probably wouldn't come back anyway. Give the poor dope a break! . . . And I thought it was a break, Jane," he added, "if that's any satisfaction to you. The absent look," he went on. "That came about ten months ago, after I was mustered out. I wasn't living dangerously any more. I was just living the way millions of guys had dreamed of living, a minor official in a very small bank—practically a clerk. That was when you began to get the absent look, sweet heart."

"All right, Alan! I don't like the way we're living. Can I help that? Does it make me some kind of criminal? During the war we were either not together at all or we were together night and day. And we lived like—like —"

"Yes. We had seven months out of five years of marriage. It was great, sweetheart, great!"

"It was. I can remember Miami as if it were yesterday . . . and the month in the Catskills—"

"Oh, hell!" he choked, and then he said no more.

The car was moving fast now, picking up speed. Alan's face was gray and hard, his mouth a thin cold line. The hard road whined under the tires. It turned sharply and the car screamed into the outer lane and pulled back slowly, gaining speed. The road straightened, the wind howled, the motor roared its complaint, and the whole world whined about their heads and caught at their breaths. Jane cried out and reached for the key, and her hand fumbled against the dark dashboard and Alan knocked it away. Her hand came down hard against a switch and the headlights went out. The road shone with a dull patina in the moonlight and the car rode the night. Jane reached out again, and Alan gripped her wrist and held it. She could feel the hand swelling. She stared out across the hood at the road that was a bright wash before them. Sudden lights blared out of the dark ahead and turned out and started toward them, moving fast. Alan's foot left the throttle and he pulled over sharply. The car was big and dark, and it hurtled by, and their car rocked with the impact of the wind . . . and something else. Jane saw it. She had thought it a shadow. But she had felt the jar behind her.

She screamed. Alan let go her wrist and slammed his foot against the brake. The car lurched sickeningly to a stop and her hands tore at the handle, and she opened the door and stumbled out and ran down the road. Alan was beside her after she had gone a little way, breathing hard, holding her, and she was leaning against him and saying, "They threw something into the car, Alan! I saw it! It looked like a dog or a child! It's there . . . in the back seat!" She stopped, trembling, and Alan held her closer, and she could feel his warm breath in her hair.

After a while he said, "Jane, there's nothing in the car. Come on. Let's go home. Let's forget everything we've said tonight, and tomorrow we'll sit down and sweat it out. Okay?"

"Please! Look in the car! Please!"

Alan stared down at her for a moment, puzzled, uncertain. Then he turned and went back to the car. She watched him open the door and lean over into the back. He straightened quickly, then leaned over again and stepped back out onto the road.

There was something in his hand, and he put it down beside him and stood staring at it.

He raised his head and said, "Janie, come up here." His voice was low, but there was a strain of excitement in it.

Jane walked back quickly. It was a leather traveling bag, a brown and beaten object, one clasp torn off.

Alan said, "There's paper in it."

"How do you know?"

"I shook it."

"Paper?"

"Yes."

"Shall we . . . open it?"

"They threw it in? That car that went past?"

"Yes."

"Maybe it fell in."

"They threw it, Alan! Open it!"

From below them in the direction of the pass, the sound of a motor faintly etched the night silence, drawing nearer. Alan picked up the bag and laid it on the front seat. He unbuckled the straps and pulled them loose, pushed open the remaining clasp at the side and hit the lock clasp with the side of his hand. It broke away and he lifted the lid. They were almost colorless in the cold moonlight, packages about an inch thick lying in a jumbled heap. Alan spoke, and he had gone beyond excitement now. His voice was level, matter-of-fact, as if he were checking a deposit.

He said, "Fifties and twenties. I'd say between sixty and a hundred thousand dollars, Jane."

Jane looked at the money for a long-drawn moment, pulling her eyes away almost with a conscious effort of will. The very stillness of it, its cool crisp cleanliness, seemed to draw her and quiet her. But she looked away and up into Alan's eyes that were deep dark shadows. She felt that she was going to cry, and she moved forward and put her face against his shoulder. His arms came tight around her.

"Oh, darling," she whispered, "I don't want to lose you."

IT was a heavy motor, the sound deepening as the car rounded one of the turns below. Jane looked at Alan and knew that he had heard it too. They both knew. They knew that this car coming toward them up the mountain was the one that was to have driven by this spot, to have cut its lights and to have felt the jar of the heavy bag as it was thrown. They moved together. Alan threw the bag onto the rear seat, lifted Jane into the car and followed her in. The car's motor turned as headlights rounded the last curve behind them. Jane looked back. The lights of the oncoming car dimmed and went out. She couldn't see it now. Alan's motor roared, choked, died, then caught. The car jumped forward. The lights of the car behind came on.

Alan saw it and picked up speed. But the grade was dropping rapidly now, twisting as it went. The car could go faster, but now it was a question of skill and compulsion. The car behind was drawing closer. They roared on. The road took a sudden drop, and below them another road crossed and pointed back toward Hollywood. Alan went into a skid at the crossing, let the car have its head and straightened up, pointed toward home. The headlights lit up the signpost, and Jane could see the name of the street: WOODROW WILSON ROAD. It was a straight road, and after a while there were no headlights behind them.

Then they were at Laurel Canyon and they turned into the southward traffic and lost themselves in the midst of it.

They were on Franklin. Alan had dropped down to Sunset and come back up to Franklin by a devious route.

He said, “No one’s following.”

“I know,” she breathed. “I know.” The car was moving slowly now, as if it felt the same exhaustion, the same spent ecstasy, that flowed through Jane with a slow soft thrumming. “It’s ours,” she whispered. “It’s ours!”

Alan said nothing. His hands gripped the wheel and gleamed white in the dim light from the dashboard. His mouth was open slightly. He licked his lips, but he still said nothing. And Jane felt a cold, uneasy tightness growing within her, knotting her stomach and pulling sharply across her lungs.

After a long while, Alan said, “We can’t keep it.”

“Why do you say that?” she asked sharply. “What’s—I don’t see—”

She stopped abruptly, bewildered. He didn’t mean it. He couldn’t mean it!

“We’ve got to get rid of it,” he repeated. “For a thousand reasons.”

“But why? It’s ours! No one in the world knows we have it!”

Once more Jane stopped, breathless. What could she say to him? A magic world lay in a dingy bag just behind her. And Alan was sitting at the wheel, his mouth slack and loose, telling her that she couldn't have it.

"If we keep it," he said evenly, "we commit a felony. In the eyes of the law, keeping it is as bad as stealing it. We could cancel ten years of our lives, and I'd never be allowed to hold a job of trust again. You want me to walk into a gamble like that absolutely blind. Jane, we can't afford to take that kind of a chance. You see that, don't you?"

Jane didn't see it. She didn't see it at all. Where was the danger? Her face was hot, and she looked up, and Alan's profile swam darkly and she fought down the searing desire to pound her fists against his face until it was without form and without words.

But Alan was still talking. She heard the word ". . . reward. Probably a pretty good-sized one for recovery," he was saying. "Maybe as much as five thousand dollars."

"Five thousand dollars!" she echoed. "Oh, Alan! I—I love you, Alan. You've got to believe that, because it's true. This is our chance, and we'll never get another. We can have what we want, and have each other too. Don't throw it away!"

He made no answer, driving slowly, staring blankly ahead. Then: "Don't you think I'd like to keep it?" he asked heavily. "But we don't know where it came from. It may be marked, it may be counterfeit, the serial numbers may be known."

"And maybe they aren't," she pleaded. "Maybe there's no way in the world to trace it. There are ways to find out things like that, especially for you. Alan, please! Compromise with me. Keep it for a week. We'll watch the papers. We'll think the whole thing over."

They were at Farrel Street, and Alan swung right. "No, Jane," he said. "If we were caught with—" His head jerked suddenly and Jane saw that he was looking into the rear-view mirror. She looked back. A single light was bearing down on them. A red light flashed on and a siren was touched lightly.

Jane screamed, "Don't stop, Alan!"

Alan pulled over to the curb, his face stiff and set. The motorcycle pulled in ahead of them and a large man in the black uniform of the city police stalked back and leaned against the car on the driver's side. His face was heavy and wide and his voice had a nasal rasp. "Lemme see your driver's license."

Alan fumbled out the license and handed it to him jerkily. The officer put his spotlight on it, looked it over, then let his eyes go past Alan to Jane. He didn't say anything, and the two of them sat in blank silence and waited. Finally the man said, "What you two so scared about?"

"Who's scared?" Alan croaked.

"You are. Didn't you ever get a ticket before?"

"Sure."

The man's eyes were small and dark. Jane saw them move and look into the back seat.

Jane's hand reached up and opened the glove compartment. He leaned over a little and flashed his light down onto the bag. He held it there.

Jane laughed and said, "We might as well tell him. He certainly doesn't care." She made her voice high and put a giddy note in it and said, "We're on our way to Las Vegas, officer. We're old-fashioned. We're eloping."

The man grinned. He turned off the flash and put it away and said, "Could be. You're still going to get a ticket. Next time you make a turn, signal. Think you can remember that?"

Alan smiled weakly and said, "I'm afraid my mind wasn't on the driving."

The officer said, "Mac, you're nervous. It's the girl that's supposed to be jittery. Get going. We'll forget about it this time."

The man handed the license back to Alan, slapped his thigh with a metal-covered book he held in his hand and walked to his motorcycle. The motor blasted angrily into the night and the man rode away. Alan turned his head slowly and looked at Jane. His eyes dropped to her right hand and his shoulders stiffened.

He stared at the thing in Jane's hand and whispered slowly, "What are you doing with that?"

Jane looked down. Her hand was tightly gripping a heavy wrench. She looked at it blankly and said nothing.

There was stridence now, and the whisper was harsh. "What did you intend to do with that?"

Jane looked up slowly. She could feel the cold wetness of her forehead, and she knew that she was white and colorless as the high moon. She said, "I didn't know I had it, Alan. I—I didn't intend to do anything with it."

Alan shuddered and raised his hands to the wheel. "Put it away," he said.

Jane put it in the compartment. Alan touched the starter and the car began to move. Jane said,

"Why didn't you tell him the money was there?"

"I don't know," he murmured. "I was just asking myself the same thing."

"You'll have to make up your mind. We'll be home in a minute. We can't leave it in the car."

He didn't answer until they were almost there. "We'll take it upstairs," he said evenly. "I want to look at it."

THE Château Michel was on Farrel below Franklin, eight stories of heavy stone with cast-stone finials, an elaborate balustrade around a steep roof, and narrow vertical windows. The windows were of amber leaded glass that effectively eliminated light and air. It was what is known in Hollywood as an apartment hotel, an apartment house with extras, one of the extras being a huge basement parking area where tenants could have their cars serviced with everything except a paint job while they slept. The night man's name was Pete, and Jane was watching for him as they pulled into their assigned space. It was about twelve feet from the stairs that led to the elevator. She didn't see Pete and they jumped out of the car and Alan put the bag on the front seat and tightened the straps. They started toward the stairs, and Pete stepped out of the line of cars ahead of them. He had a wet chamois in one hand.

He said, " You folks been away?"

Jane smiled and said, "No. Some things Mr. Palmer had in storage."

Alan walked on in silence and Jane said good night to Pete and gave him a warm smile. The two elevators were automatic after six P.M. Jane pushed the button and stood waiting. Alan pushed the button again and cursed quietly, and Jane found that she was having difficulty with her breathing. Alan was pale and his eyes were blank.

The elevator came and took them in and grumbled upward to the seventh floor. In the hall, Jane said, "Kathy! You said she was coming in for coffee."

"She's probably in bed."

They walked down the hall, and hot little fingers jabbed at Jane, and her scalp felt tight. Kathy was Alan's younger sister, and her apartment was only two doors down from theirs. How did Alan know whether she was in bed or not? Or if she was asleep? He could be indifferent about it. Jane couldn't. She hurried down and unlocked the door and held it open until Alan was through. She closed it and locked it again and leaned against the door. Alan went on into the bedroom. She waited, but he didn't come out again and there was no sound.

Jane ran into the room. It was dark there, but the light from the living room showed her the bag on the floor beside the bed and Alan lying on the blue silk spread with his arm across his eyes. Jane snapped on the bedside lamp and lay down beside him gently. She brought her fingers down across his cheek, pushed them up again and gently nudged at the arm across his eyes.

Alan looked at her then and put his arms around her and pulled her against him. He whispered, "Janie, Janie. You're so unbelievably beautiful. The weapons are all on your side. There's no fight left."

"What do you want to do with it, Alan?"

His face twisted. "I don't know. I want it. I'd like to keep it. I could make it work for us for the rest of our lives. But it's a rat race, Jane. A blind alley with a big barred gate at the end!"

"Darling, we can hide it someplace where no one can connect us with it. And we won't touch it until we know we can do it, until we know we're safe and we've worked out every tiny detail. If we can't do it, we'll just forget it! We could even let the police know where it was in some way, so it would-n't be wasted."

His face was dark and his eyes were bright. It was a long time before he answered. "All right, Jane. God help us, but we'll hold it for a while."

She raised her shoulders and put her lips against his. They didn't hear the knock until it had come again with an urgent insistence. They sat up, silent and still.

Jane whispered, "It's Kathy."

"No. She'd try the door."

They waited, the hope palpable between them: Perhaps it wouldn't come again. But it came again, more loudly. Jane leaped up and pushed the bag far under the bed.

Alan turned off the light and whispered, "Don't answer it."

"We've got to!" She went out of the bedroom and closed the door. She walked to the living-room door and stood there trembling. She told herself that it couldn't be about the money. It couldn't be. No one knew they had it. She opened the door.

Pete was standing there, looking worried and apologetic. He said, "I didn't figure you'd had time to get to bed yet." He held out a key. "You folks went off and left your motor running. Here's the key."

"How careless. Thank you, Pete. Thanks very much." He gave her a puzzled look, nodded and turned away. She closed the door and stood there looking at the key and realizing that she was still trembling. She heard Alan come out of the bedroom. She turned. He was pale now and his mouth was pulled down tight. He walked through to the kitchen without looking at her, and she could hear him mixing drinks. He brought out two highballs, handed her one and asked her to sit down. He waited until she was settled on the chesterfield and sat down across from her.

"That did it," he said. "The thing almost had me for a minute—the idea of keeping the money, I mean. But we were scared, Jane. And that's how it would be. We'd be forever afraid of every knock at the door. When the phone rang, we'd look at each other and wonder. We'd jump at every sound. The money would lie somewhere and we'd think we were all-fired rich. And we wouldn't ever be able to spend it. It would knock all our values to hell and we'd live in fear . . . and we'd never be able to touch it!"

"Don't, Alan! We were wrong to be afraid. No one in the world knows where that money is but you and me."

Alan stared at her and his mouth was twisted. "No?" he said quietly. "How about the man who threw the money in? I don't know what the setup was, but it seems logical he'd take a good look at us."

"He couldn't have. Our lights were off and he

was going too fast."

"And there's the car that followed us. Maybe he wasn't a part of it, but I think he was. He got a good look at us, maybe even the license—and how many new convertibles painted a nice bright yellow are there in this area? They could find us that way. And they will when they discover the mistake they made."

"What if they do? We'll have it hidden. It's ours, darling. I don't care if we have to wait a year before we start using it. I'll wait gladly."

"Stop it, Jane! You're going to dream yourself right into Tehachapi. Wouldn't it be great if the papers carried a description of that suitcase tomorrow? The cop saw it. Pete had a better look at it. I can see him reading his morning paper and remembering that we acted kind of queer, left our motor running. And we had a battered brown bag!"

Jane took hold of her lip with her bright straight teeth and bit. She bit hard, because she had to keep from telling Alan that it was true: They had acted queer; he had. They had left the motor running; he had. They had been stopped by a policeman, because he had failed to signal. Alan, Alan! She closed her eyes and felt the pain and thought of the money lying in the brown bag and made herself face it—she had to carry Alan. She couldn't do it alone. He wouldn't let her. She had to keep him with her.

She said, "Alan, my own bag is brown. It's in good condition and it isn't quite so large as the other one. But we could do something about its condition, and no one would be able to claim—if it ever came to that—that my bag wasn't the one they saw."

Alan thought about that, and Jane pressed on, "There are a hundred things to think about, darling. But there are answers. We can win, darling. The whole world's in there, Alan. We've just got to be a little smarter than the rest. And we can be. Between us, we'll beat them all!"

Alan looked suddenly tired. "Pep talks now," he said. "Listen, Jane. How do you hide a hundred thousand dollars? And if you solve that one, how do you spend a hundred thousand dollars? Let's assume we've got it all clear. It isn't counterfeit, it isn't marked--"

Jane rose suddenly, turned and ran into the bedroom and pulled the bag from under the bed. She opened it and took out one of the packs and went back into the living room and threw it onto the chesterfield. "Look at it, Alan. Is it . . . counterfeit?"

Alan didn't get up. He sat and stared at her and said, "One more step, one more link in the chain. Paper takes fingerprints. You've just put yours all over those bills."

"I'll wipe them off. Are they counterfeit, Alan? Are they marked?"

He came over and sat down and poked at them with the end of his pencil. It was a packet of twenties, and turned one over with the pencil and studied it closely. He picked it up gingerly by the corners and carried over to the light and looked at it from a half dozen angles. He brought it back and dropped it, looked at a few more casually, and sat down on the chesterfield.

He said, "I'm no expert, Jane. But they look like

the real thing to me. And the numbers aren't consecutive. It's old money, and there aren't any marks on it that I could see." Resignation sounded through the level tones, as if he had bowed quietly to some bedeviled and ineluctable logic. He said faintly, "But I work in a bank. I can't suddenly blossom out a rich man."

"We won't touch the money! Not until we know—until we know that it's safe and we can use it without risk. Just help me hide it, dearest, and after that we'll let you decide what's best."

After a long while, he said, "We'll keep it. We'll keep it one week. Then we'll decide whether we ought to give it up. We'll hide it tonight."

"Where?" Breathlessly.

"At Union Station. We'll check it. They handle a million bags and a million faces. They don't take names. They just hand you a ticket."

"How long will they keep it before they—"

"Indefinitely, I think. They have a warehouse they take it to if you leave it too —"

He didn't finish, because Jane had thrown herself down beside him. She pulled his head down and her fingers played softly in his hair. Outside, a horn blasted into the night and someone shouted and the night was silent again.

THE great station was crowded and people moved urgently in a dozen directions, or stood about with weary patience, or slept in awkward helplessness in the deep leather seats that filled the long waiting room. Two men were on duty at the check stand, working rapidly, handling the baggage as if it contained clothing and toilet articles and souvenirs, looking at a face only now and then to answer a question.

Jane had taken the bag from the apartment by going down the back stairs and out the side entrance, where Alan had picked her up. Now Alan had the bag and Jane was waiting at the magazine stand, watching him while she nervously riffled the pages of a twenty-five-cent reprint. He was wearing a hat and the brim was turned down all around. It looked strange, absurd. Jane told herself it was because he just never wore a hat, that he wouldn't look strange to anyone else. It was his turn at the counter now, and he lifted the bag with a stiff movement, and Jane remembered that he was wearing gloves. Fingerprints, he had said. But it was a warm night. And the topcoat, with the collar turned up! She was holding the book tightly now, and her face was hot. It was clear to anyone with eyes that Alan was about to check a suitcase containing a hundred thousand dollars!

The little dark man behind the counter took the bag, and it seemed to Jane that Alan spoke to him. The man looked up and said something, handed Alan a white ticket and turned. Alan walked away, toward the great doors, and Jane put the book into its place on the rack and hurried outside. She found Alan in the car, lighting a cigarette. His hands shook. He had forgotten to take off the gloves. She put her arms around his waist and held tight to him, and after a while the tensions that had been building in her were gone and she began the ascent again.

"It's all right now, isn't it, darling?"

Alan said, "Yeh, I guess so."

"Where's the ticket?"

He handed it to her. It was white, about two inches square, with a paragraph of fine writing and a six-digit number. Jane said, "You keep it, darling."

He took it and put it in the side pocket of the topcoat. "There's a hole in the pocket," he said. "It'll slide down in the lining and stay there until we want to use it or put it somewhere else." He threw the cigarette away and started the car.

"What's the matter, lover?"

He didn't answer. The car turned out onto Aliso and started west toward home.

Then Alan said, "The money's there now, and no one will ever know who put it there. Now let's forget it, Jane, shall we? Let's just forget it!"

"What did you say to the man at the counter?"

"I didn't say anything to the man at the counter."

"But—" Jane stopped, and something touched her coldly. "You did. I saw you."

"Oh, yes. I told him I was going to a hospital for a while and wouldn't be picking up the bag for some time. He said it would be all right."

The bright pattern suddenly broke and the quick thought was there, spread out thinly in her mind: Alan was lying.

KATHERINE PALMER folded the leavened egg whites into the rich batter with the slow care and infinite concentration of one who handles fissionable material. Her full dark brows pulled together and a tiny pink tongue tip protruded uneasily from between her teeth. She looked unhappy. Actually she was not only happy but contented. She enjoyed the simple act of making waffles because Jay had shown her how, including in the recipe a kind of esoterica out of the folklore of America. Jay, who was going to marry her, and who had died in the shallow crimson waters off Normandy. If the pains she was taking now were for Jay, the thought didn't occur to her. These were for her brother, of whom she was quietly and unobtrusively fond, and for his wile Jane, whom she liked because she thought Jane was beautiful.

She was young, but not quite so young as she looked. It was not that she was a small girl or that she had flour across her nose. It lay in her warm olive skin and in an expression of winsome perplexity, which was entirely a matter of the way her eyes were made and the dark brows grew, and had nothing to do with the quality of her psyche.

She gave the fluffy mixture in the golden crock a last fold and turned to open the refrigerator door.

A brief and somewhat systematized rattling sounded from the front door and a voice called, "Hey, Shorty, the Sunday-morning muffins ready yet?"

Pretty quick, Alan; sit down. . . Morning, Jane!"

There was no answer, and she wiped her hands and stepped out into the living room. "Isn't Jane — Oh, I was afraid you hadn't come, Janie."

Jane had sat down with some newspapers on her lap and was already busy with one of them. "Oh, yes," she said absently, "on Sundays we have breakfast with Kathy."

Kathy caught her breath shortly and then

smiled. "There's an added feature this morning—ham juice by name. It's cream poured over the ham while it's cooking. 'S good."

"Bring 'er on," Alan grinned. "Need any help?"

"Not allowed."

She started back to the kitchen, and Alan said, "Coming to the show with us tonight?"

The question took Kathy by surprise. She had made it a point to avoid intruding on Alan's and Jane's life together, and almost never went with them on their evenings out. She would have liked to go tonight, but she turned to make an excuse, and Jane brought a hand sharply down across the paper in her lap.

"You and Kathy go," she said tightly. "I just can't take any more Sunday movies."

"No-o," Kathy said quietly. "I can't make it tonight. Excuse me; I have to look at the ham!"

She fled to the tiny kitchen and stood staring down into the yellow batter, searching for an answer. Had she said something to offend Jane? Then she noticed that the batter was losing its airy lightness, and she forgot Jane in her anxiety to get breakfast under way before it was too late. She began to move quickly, precisely, only vaguely aware of a sibilant sound of voices in the other room. A slammed door put a period to the sounds, and Kathy stopped abruptly, waiting. She looked into the silent living room.

Jane was facing the closed door, standing with a listening stillness. Then she walked to the door and stepped out and closed it behind her. Kathy turned and sat down at the breakfast table and swallowed past a growing tightness in her throat.

She wouldn't cry, but she felt a need to cry. Not because her breakfast was spoiled or that she must eat alone, but because some sudden and dreadful thing had come between Alan and Jane. She knew her brother well. She knew that nothing else could account for what had happened.

Jane hesitated a moment at her own door, composing herself, reminding herself that she must keep Alan with her at any cost. She opened the door timidly and stood just inside the room, like a small girl called into her father's study.

"I'm sorry, Alan. Terribly sorry." She walked toward him slowly. "It may have seemed petty to you, but it's actually important. I don't like to go and sit in the dark and watch other people live. I don't want to have other people do my living for me. I'm just not made that way!"

He turned his back and picked up a cigarette and lit it with clumsy fingers. Jane moved around beside him, and his face was dark and hard, and his eyes looked hot. He dropped the match and picked it up again and broke it.

She said, almost shyly, "Alan, what's wrong? It isn't just that I didn't want to go to a show tonight. I know it isn't."

"I don't think we'd better talk about it right now."

"Please, Alan."

He had been pacing jerkily in front of the chesterfield. He stopped now and said, "How much money have you spent in the last four days?"

She laughed and said, "Oh, Alan, surely not that."

"I'll tell you," he said, and his voice was tight;

"three hundred and eighty dollars. Exactly thirty per cent of our entire account. In four days!"

There was more coming. Jane knew that, and she waited for it. She took conscious rein on herself and said quietly, "Alan, it's less than one half of one per cent of the money we have."

His face was suddenly pale, the lines around his mouth like scars. "We were going to leave it down there. Forget it! Now you're spending it like mad and keeping books on it and being quietly patient with me because I seem to think it's a little unreasonable." He broke the cigarette in a tray and began the pacing again.

"But nothing's happened, Alan. There's been nothing in the papers. We're sure now the money's ours. And I only bought things I've needed for a long time."

"Sit down, will you, Jane? I've got to talk to you."

She walked over to the chesterfield and stood looking at him for a moment. She sat down. He began quietly enough, but the strain in his voice was like a sickness. "I've watched you now for four days—yes, and four nights—walking around like a zombie. I've heard you when you got out of bed and paced around in here. Last night I counted it. You stayed in bed exactly two hours."

"Of course. I'm nervous. We're both nervous."

"Yes, we're both nervous. I'm probably more nervous about this than you are. But it isn't nervousness that makes you walk, Jane. I don't know what it is. I don't want to know. It's whatever that money has done to you. I've tried to tell myself not to let it get me. I remind myself that I work in a bank, that I'm used to handling bags full of money without getting the idea they're mine. But it hasn't done any good to tell myself that."

Jane said, "Alan, I don't understand what you're trying to say to me."

He looked at her for a long while, and the sickness was in his eyes now. "I'm disgusted. That's what I'm trying to say. I'm trying to say that I never knew you until . . . this happened. I keep thinking what an empty shell of a human being you are. I hear you walking around all night long. It's got so I think about you the way I think of people who take dope. The money is your dope. You're all hopped up with it. Or maybe you walk the floors at night because the money's down there. It's way down at Union Station, instead of here, under your bed where you can count it. The money—"

"Stop it!" She put her hand to her mouth and looked at him wildly over it. "Because I know what the money could mean to us, I'm a hophead! Because I'm sick with dread that we might lose it, I'm—" She put her face in her hands and shook her head, and the soft blond hair fell coolly down across her arms and quieted her and she said no more.

After a while she looked up. Alan had dropped into the wing chair across from her, his face slack, eyes spent and flecked, and two spots of color burning high in his cheeks.

"Anyway," he breathed, "the problem is ended. We're not keeping the money."

"Don't I have anything to say about that?"

"I've gone with you a long way, Jane. Much too far," he said quietly. "I wish I could say 'Go ahead and take it,' but I can't. When you get caught, I'm caught. If I never touched a cent of it, I'd be just as guilty as you. And you'd be caught, Jane. Apparently they're keeping a hush on the money. You'll never know whether it's hot money or not, until you try to spend some of it and they tap you on the shoulder and take you away.

"But even if the money is all right, you couldn't spend it the way you want. The world's too complicated, Jane. People would begin to move in on you: The sheriff's office, the city police, the FBI, every hawkshaw in the world with an unsolved case involving missing funds or property would get interested in how you got your money. They'd hear about you, Jane, somehow. The Internal Revenue Bureau would begin to pry, and they'd end up asking for a look at your income records. You'd have to have more than a nice smile and a good story for them. They'd want to know where you got it, and when, and from whom. So you'd have to keep it hidden, where it would be safe, but where you could get at it and where a search warrant wouldn't find it. Can you think of a place like that?" He closed his eyes. It was the longest speech he had ever made.

Jane said, "I've thought of all that, Alan. Those people can be bought off. They all have a price. We could go to Las Vegas. We could make an arrangement with one of the gambling houses there. It would cost a little, but they'd be glad to let us seem to win several thousand dollars, and they could take it off their income tax. That's just one way. There are others. And why is there a problem about hiding it? What you put into a safe-deposit box is your own business."

Alan opened his eyes and looked at her admiringly. He said, "Not entirely true, but you've been thinking. That's what you do when you walk the floors. But everyone doesn't have a price, Jane. Don't ever forget that."

"Yes, I've been thinking. I've been thinking for both of us, Alan!" Her voice broke and she ran over to him and knelt beside him. "I don't want to lose you, darling. You've got to stay with me now. I don't want it any other way."

Alan looked down at her and Jane searched his face anxiously, but there was no warmth there and no response. It was just tired and cold. He moved her hand off his knee and stood up.

He said, "Listen, Jane. I've been doing some thinking too. Not about the money. I've forgotten the money. I told you I'd wait a week, and I will. Next Wednesday we're going to drop that ticket in an envelope, type out an explanation and send it to the district attorney's office." He laughed. "That's one of the things that's so nice about this. We can't even claim a reward now. But that isn't what I've been thinking about, Jane. While you spent your nights pacing around in the living room, I thought about you, and about what you said to me driving home from Burbank. Can you remember, Jane? It was a long time ago, before we latched onto that brown bag. Before that little fortune was dropped into our laps you were going to leave me. You had just given me the pitch. And I was thinking of taking you and me and the new car for a power dive off one of the Mulholland cliffs. Well, Jane, that's the main reason I'm not keeping the money. Because it would mean keeping you. And I don't want to keep you."

The words had been quiet and without passion, but Jane had known before they were spoken what Alan was going to say. She had hardly heard the words. She was still kneeling beside the chair, looking up at him, and his face was swimming in a great hot blur, and she could feel herself rising and words welling up until they choked her. But she didn't rise and the words were never spoken and she gripped the chair and looked at her hand lying limply on the floor. Her eyes began to burn and then were wet, and when she looked up again there was wetness on her face and the taste of salt on her lips.

Alan gazed down at her. Surprise and vague uncertainty lay behind his eyes. He said nothing at all.

Jane said, "It's all right, Alan. I can't . . . blame you. If you still feel the same way when Wednesday comes, I won't try to stop you. I—" But she was crying. She put her face in the chair, and sobs shook her and rode over her and she could hear a wailing in her ears that she knew was hers and that she could do nothing about.'

Alan was beside her now, and she felt herself lifted suddenly and swiftly and held close, and lips were kissing her where the tears were and her arms were around Alan, holding tight. The slow ebbing of the sobs and the clawing of breath and Alan's lips on her eyes. Alan's whisper that he loved her almost but not quite erased the memory of his words, "I'm not keeping the money."

PART TWO

THE evening was warm, the Sunday traffic slow and patient on Wilshire. The Palmers were in search of something they had lost. That was the way Alan, in a rare moment of sentiment, had put it, and the place they were going was Alan's idea: McPhearson Park, for a sail on the lake. They weren't quite sure whether that was the first thing they had done together when they first met, but it had been sandwiched in fairly early among the more common things that flying men did on a ten-day leave.

They walked down the path toward the bright pavilion, hearing the quiet sounds of the boats on the lake, smelling the heavy odor of shoestring potatoes, ten cents a bag. Inside there were empty stools at the fountain, and they stopped there and had a sundae. The girl behind the counter was blond and young and red-cheeked, with an eager smile and a willingness to talk. Alan asked her if anything had changed about the lake since the war. She said she didn't rightly know, since she had been in grammar school in Wichita before the war. Alan laughed and told her that her words had officially consigned him to middle age. They finished their sundaes and went down the steep flight of wooden stairs to the landing.

The lake was the trysting place of a large part of Los Angeles' more callow population, but it was too early yet for them. Now, in the early evening, many of the boats still carried adults with children on their laps. Alan paid a deposit and got a ticket for one of the motorboats, and while they waited he talked with the basque-shirted boy who handled the loading. Jane looked off across the lake and relaxed for a moment from the strain of sharing Alan's mood.

In a little while they were on the lake. The boat was made for privacy—high sides, a canvas top—the lake a dark and enchanted place. Jane lay back with her head against Alan's shoulder, the boat moving silently on its electric motor, Alan holding the wheel with the touch of his hand and telling Jane that everything was going to be all right; that, as a matter of fact, he was thinking seriously of getting his commercial license. More pay, no humdrum, and he'd be flying again.

Jane stared off across the cold hard surface of the water. She shuddered, and Alan held her closer and asked if she was cold. She shook her head and Alan talked again of his plans. But Jane did not hear the words. They impinged upon the surface of her mind and altered and hardened and became other words that thrust at her over and over again, *I'm not keeping the money. It would mean keeping you. I'm not keeping—*

Everything was going to be all right.

The black and dimpled water stirred suddenly as a brief wind rippled across it, and Jane found herself recalling another time, another stretch of waters. The autumn wind lowered across the Arkansas River and cut sharply at the girl standing on the bridge. The girl was tall and thin, and she was not pretty. There was a hump in the thin nose that sharpened the face. She was sixteen years old, and her name was Jane Petry. She looked at the water in the way that people do who are wondering how it will feel when it folds over them and their dreams and the things that brought them there. She stood and leaned against the cold wet metal of the guard rail. As she stood there, in her mind she visualized herself climbing the rail, clinging to it a moment and jumping. She anticipated how long the drop would be, and how the water would bite, and how her throat would scream against the seal of waters. And out of that infinity of imagined deaths, Jane Petry found new terms on which to live.

She left school, and within the week she was working. She claimed to be eighteen and found a job as a switchboard operator in Tulsa's largest realty firm. She lived ascetically and worked with sober and passionless precision. She was never late. She was never absent. In six months she was operating the Monster, a great complex bookkeeping machine, and she was earning thirty-five dollars a week and saving twenty-seven of it.

At the end of the first year she wrote to the California Medical Association and asked for the names of the best plastic surgeons in California. She wrote them all, and made her arrangements with one in Los Angeles. She left Tulsa when she was nineteen with a bag full of bare essentials, thirty-five hundred dollars and a plan. She took a room in a dark walk-up hotel on Alvarado and called on her doctor. He was a good doctor. Some of the world's best people looked down noses which he had fashioned. He told her that because she was alone, she would have to make arrangements for a bed in a hospital. Jane didn't want that. She had planned carefully, and there were other places for the money. Jane invented a sister, and the doctor insisted she have the sister with her the day of the operation.

Jane hired a girl to be with her on that day, and she lost the hump in her nose. She went back to her hotel in a cab and the hired sister left her there and went away. Jane lay in the dark room, the pain dull at first, like soft hammers beating behind her eyes. And then the pain was agony, and delirium came with the night. The Monster rode the delirium, clattering and sending out great spirals of figures that she totaled over and over in mounting frenzy, and the totals were forever wrong and the figures were an endless torment. But Jane dressed her wound and bathed her body and brought herself back to her doctor each day for ten frightful days, until the agony was gone.

And Jane had received the first installment on her dream: a new nose, a beautiful flawless face.

Now Jane shopped; not with a breathless immediacy or as a means of expression, but soberly, carefully, taking no special pleasure in the act itself. She bought where the buying was best and sewed labels from the Wilshire shops into purchases from downtown stores. In the evenings she went to school and learned something of California's complex laws of community property, and of divorce.

And when the rains came she went to Palm Springs. Two months later she was Mrs. Michael Blanchard, and, not long after, she found that her dream had collapsed abruptly about her. She had first seen Blanchard at a Palm Springs casino. He had dropped a fifty-dollar chip, had watched it roll under a table with a kind of amused abstraction, and had ignored it. He was in his late fifties, and she had learned that he was a free-lance director. It was only later that Jane understood this was a kindly way of saying that he was unemployed. And later yet she understood that his was a profession in which unemployment was pernicious and incurable. He had—

Jane winced, her head turning suddenly to the side, as if she had been slapped. This was an old wound. She found now, as she had found in past reflections on this first marriage, that she could not probe too deeply here without dropping an involuntary curtain across her mind. The truant wind returned and Jane whispered into it soundlessly that she had betrayed Jane Petry. The war had come. The gay bright people had run for cover. And she had married Alan. She had betrayed the girl who had lain for days and nights that were a babbling eternity of madness, who had lived the dusty dedicated years—

Everything was going to be all right.

IT was seven-thirty on Monday morning and Alan was standing at the door, ready to leave. Jane went to him and kissed him, and Alan said, "We're not licked, are we, honey?"

"Not us."

"I wonder if everybody lives as cockeyed a life behind their doors as we do, Jane?"

"I doubt it."

"Well, they probably think they do."

"Probably."

"Well, hold the fort."

He went out and closed the door. Jane leaned against it for a moment, then ran in and threw herself on the bed and buried her face in a pillow and cried. She cried because somewhere—at the lake or in the sleepless night—there had been cast up a cold resolve that frightened her. She lay there until the morning sun rose high and warmed the room, and the commonplace sounds from the street had reassured her.

She bathed quickly and began to clean the apartment. She knew that she could not think of the thing that was pressing itself upon her unless a part of her mind was occupied with the problem of dust on the coffee table, unless the thinking was accompanied by the complacent drone of a vacuum cleaner. By noon she was hungry, and in the midst of her eating she realized that the important thing was done, and that it was somehow right. Whatever followed now was a matter of incident. The decision had been made. She did not know when or how. It had been taken without thought, rising out. of a need that was beyond thought. She had done nothing. But it was too late now to turn back. She felt a calm and a peace that she had felt only once before. When she had walked away from the bridge in Tulsa.

The knock came at two o'clock—a heavy knock that was repeated impatiently before Jane got to the door and opened it. He was a young man, probably not yet thirty, neither tall nor short, and he was lean. He looked at Jane for a while out of sharp gray eyes set in a pale face. He had a thin dark mustache riding an even thinner smile, and he was holding a wallet. He flipped the wallet open, held it out for a few seconds and put it into a hip pocket.

"Fuller," he said, "detective bureau." His voice was also thin, pitched high, as if it had adapted itself to his lean body and his quick, birdlike movements.

Jane felt the blood begin to pound, and she knew that it would show in a moment in a column of color rising in her throat. She fought it down and felt her face grow cold, and she said, "What is it?"

"Does Mr. Alan Palmer live here?"

"I am Mrs. Palmer. My husband is at work." She managed to get a note of righteousness into her voice. She felt better. The money was hidden, the ticket was with Alan in his topcoat. She could carry it off.

"We're making a routine check, Mrs. Palmer, on the owners of new convertibles painted cream or yellow."

"We have one. It's yellow."

"Might I come in, Mrs. Palmer?" She hesitated a moment and said, "Of course." She stepped aside and closed the door behind him. He walked into the living room and looked around slowly, taking in the place with a casual eye. Jane walked to the chesterfield and sat down.

He said, "Mrs. Palmer, would you mind if I looked your place over a bit?" Jane crossed her legs and let the dress pull up over her knee. She said, "Why?"

He smiled. It was wider now, and it was taking things for granted that Jane didn't like having taken for granted. She wondered if the smile, the dark mustache, the lean body, were what women would consider a nice combination. He wasn't an ugly man. He was even possibly handsome. She smiled back at him and tried to make it warm. She knew it looked pale and a little sick.

He said, "I'm sure you haven't anything to hide, have you?"

"Yes, an untidy bedroom."

Mr. Fuller let the smile relax slowly. "I'd like to look around a little. Do you let me or no?"

Jane lowered her eyes and wet her lips and let them part just a little. "Don't you usually have warrants or something for this kind of thing?" She made it sound polite and friendly, and she followed it with the smile, warmer now.

"No. But I'd be happy to go and get you one."

"If I let you look around, will you tell me what it's all about? It'll give me something to make small talk with at bridge tonight."

"Sure, Mrs. Palmer, sure. Want to go around with me or do you trust me alone?"

"That's the only way I would trust you, Mr. Fuller—alone."

He grinned and went into the bedroom. She heard the sound of the porcelain lid in the bathroom being lifted, then dropped; the echoing sound of the shower door being slammed shut; the almost indistinct noise of springs, as if the mattress had been raised and lowered carefully. Then he was in the kitchen opening doors and drawers, lifting the lid on the Dutch oven, looking into boxes with their crisp paper wrappings.

He came back in and sat down on the chesterfield beside her and looked at her with a pale, fixed stare for a long while. He said, "Where'd you hide it, gorgeous?"

Her face was suddenly cold and stiff, and she heard herself saying, "Hide? Hide what?"

"The money, Mrs. Palmer. You shouldn't have let me go through your place. If you were an innocent little housewife with nothing to hide but the iceman, you wouldn't have let me have a peep. You'd have been screaming for a warrant and a lawyer, and sending wires to your congressman."

Jane stared at him blankly, gaining time, knowing that the blank stare could mean anything. She was trying to work it out. The man had dropped out of character. He seemed more like someone working for himself than a city employee on a routine check.

She said, "Aren't your methods a little unorthodox, Mr. Fuller?"

"We have to use angles to get results. It worked fine in your case, for instance."

"How was that?"

"You're about to tell me what you did with the dough, as soon as you get through being wise. When I asked you where the money was, your eyes gave you away like a pair of goads."

"Goads? What's a goad?"

"Crooked dice, honey."

Jane laughed.

He said. "There's nothing funny about this. I hope I don't have to prove it to you."

There wasn't any doubt about it now. Jane said,

"What did you say your name was?" He repeated the name, and she stood up and walked to the phone. He sat and watched her. She dialed information and asked for the number of the city detective bureau. She waited, hung up and began to dial again. He stood up then and came over to the phone and pushed the bar down. She put the receiver down over his fingers and he drew them away.

"You've got quite a flair, beautiful. I like you. Too bad you're a chiseler."

Jane walked back to the chesterfield. Without Alan on her side, and only two days more. She couldn't fight this man. Not now. She needed him. He knew where the money came from. And also—At the lake last night she had looked down at the dark water, and a swift thought had slipped past her mind with a chill insinuation. It was still a vague shadow, but it was taking form, and there was excitement in it.

She waved at the chair across from her and said, "Sit down. I want to talk to you."

"I don't mind if I do." He sat down beside her, and Jane moved over to the end, so that she could turn and look at him.

She said, "You were too good-looking to be a detective."

"Thanks," he said dryly. "After I was sure you had the dough, I stopped trying. I knew I'd get it out of you."

"I don't have it."

"Please, gorgeous, let us not haggle."

"We're not going to. My husband has the money and he hasn't told me where he put it . . .

yet." She smiled and dropped her eyes to his mouth and let her lips fall open again.

"Nice story. I like that trick with your eyes and mouth too. It does things for me." He moved closer and put a hand on her knee. She took the hand away. He said, "Tut, tut. That look was for a reason. I'm just taking my cue like a gentleman."

"You're taking it a little too fast." She wrinkled her nose at him.

"Isn't that what you wanted?"

"Why should I?"

"You probably think you've got reasons. You don't have. I'm just a small-time grifter, honey. Everything I've got in the world is wherever you put it."

"That's not small time."

"I was just graduating when you spoiled it."

"How much money is there in that bag?"

"Don't you know?"

"Did you see where the liquor was when you were in the kitchen?"

"Sure."

"Go make us a drink."

"You're not stalling, are you?" He grinned. "Hubby won't be home until later. I made an appointment to see him at the bank . . . about opening an account. I wanted to be sure to be alone with you."

Jane leaned forward quickly and put her head against the back of the chesterfield about three inches from his face. "Please," she said. "I don't have the money. I want it, and to get it, I need help. Go make us a drink and we'll talk about it."

He didn't move away. He looked down at her

across his nose, and she could feel his warm breath on her lips. He didn't say anything, and after a while he stood up and went into the kitchen, and Jane forced her mind to turn, coldly filling in the outline of the idea, checking the details, looking for error. She shuddered because there was hazard in it, and a need for courage. But there was also perfection, because there was simplicity, and because error could mean disaster. And there was no time! No time to find a better way.

He came back with two drinks, ill-made and raw, and they sat with them for a while, saying nothing. Finally he whispered, "The dough is mine. Maybe you need help to get it. I don't."

"What do I call you besides Stupid, Mr. Fuller?"

"Stupid will do. If you get tired of that, you can try Danny." He took an untidy drink. "But you aren't subtle, gorgeous. I turn up, and you decide I've got to be stalled. So you give me a quickie about not knowing where the dough is, and needing my help to get it. Tsk-tsk."

Jane looked at him admiringly and whispered, "All right, I lied to you about that. I do know where the money is, but I haven't it, and I want it. And we have precious little time. My husband will turn the money over to the police at the drop of a hat. He intends to do it in two days in any case. He promised me he'd keep it that long."

Danny Fuller was listening now.

"So don't you see?" she went on. "You can't possibly get it without my help, and I need yours."

"It's just a two-day drag, huh?"

She shook her head. "We'll get it tomorrow."

"How?"

"I don't know yet. I'll work something out. I've got to."

Danny Fuller looked at her wistfully. "You know," he said, "I think you will."

Jane nodded distantly. "I don't intend to let it gel away from me."

"From us, you mean," Danny said, then whispered, "You know, I've never got half this close to anything as beautiful as you. How come? How come you don't exploit that face and that figure? Like the man says, you oughta be in the movies."

Jane flushed, and wondered why, and decided it was because it had been just the right thing to do. She raised her eyes to Danny's face, and his eyes were bright and he reached out and pulled her against him and put his lips hard against hers. She yielded for a moment, and Danny brought his hand up across her slender waist. She stiffened and pushed away.

"What's your name, gorgeous?"

"Jane."

"Well, Jane, I'm going to need some incentive to give you half of what happens to be all mine."

"We divide it even, h'm?"

"Yuh, that's the way us denizens do these things, you know."

"Do I get any guaranty that I actually get my half?"

He frowned suddenly and pushed her aside. He stood up and walked toward the door. Jane followed him, and he turned and said, "Sorry, gorgeous, but the small talk all of a sudden got under my skin. I keep remembering you're a chiseler. Where do I see you tomorrow?"

"I'll have to be able to call you."

He thought about that for a while, took out a card and wrote a telephone number on it. "Call that number between five and five-thirty tomorrow. And for your sake, beautiful, I hope you're not trying to soft-song me." He opened the door and walked away.

THE next day Jane went shopping. She left early, a few moments after Alan had gone, because there were things to do, and all of them demanded perfection and care and thought. At no time during this day must she be hurried or pressed for time or touched by doubt.

She shopped in downtown Los Angeles, wearing an old dark coat and a turban. In a ten-cent store she bought some horn-rimmed glasses and put them on. She couldn't see too well with them, but she could get along. In another store she bought a small flashlight. She could have found a flashlight in the first store, but Jane wasn't doing that on this day. In a sporting-goods store she bought some heavy line for deep-sea fishing. The man who waited on her was tanned and handsome and infinitely bored. He looked at her in the absent way that she could remember—the way men had looked at her when she had had a bump in her nose. She felt flushed and angry when he was counting out her change. She thought wildly of going out and taking off the hideous turban and the glasses, and coming back and telling him she had forgotten something. But she could come back some other time with a mink coat on.

She found a hardware store and asked for some

sash weights. The girl behind the counter wanted to know what she meant. Jane explained that they were heavy, six or seven pounds, about ten inches long, an inch or so thick. The girl didn't think they had any, and Jane tried two other stores and finally found some in a junk shop on Third Street. She bought four. Outside the shop she took them out of the sack and put them in her handbag. She tucked it under her arm and walked the seven blocks to the bus station on Hill Street.

Going home she removed the glasses and slipped them between the seat and the side of the bus. But she continued to carry the bag with its twenty-eight pounds of iron. Her shoulder burned and the muscles in her arm were numb, but she had to get used to it. She had to carry it as if it contained a powder puff and a lipstick and an assortment of bobby pins.

At home she locked the door and took the handbag into the bedroom. She cut the fishing line into four pieces and put it in the bag with the weights, hid it under some slips in the bottom drawer of her chest and went out again. She had to find an alley or a back lot, a place for a yellow car to sit for several hours without attracting attention. Seven blocks up Farrel she found a vacant lot with a great billboard on it set at an angle against a five-story building.

Between the building and the board there would be just room enough for the convertible, and no one would be able to see it.

She walked back home. She locked the door again and went into the bedroom and took Alan's dark suit from the closet. It had been tailored at a small shop in Hollywood. She cut the threads that held the label and pulled the label off. A cleaner's tag was stapled on the inside pocket of the coat and another on the waistband of the trousers. She pulled them off and looked carefully for more marks or labels. There were none, and she took the pieces of cloth and sent them down the drain and hung the suit back up again. She looked through his shirts and underclothes until she found some that had no laundry marks on them. She laid these out on the bed. At the bottom of his chest of drawers, tucked away at the back, was his service automatic. It was wrapped in flannel, oiled and shiny, the clip full. She put the gun into the pocket of her coat. It was a heavy gun and the barrel was long. It wedged tightly into the pocket and pulled the coat down on one side. She rearranged it on the hanger. It was all right. The gun didn't show.

The next two hours were the hardest because there was nothing to do, nothing to think about. She had done all the planning and the thinking, and there was nothing now but simple movement. At one minute after five she called the number Danny had given her. The dull sound of the ring came twice and a high-pitched voice piped, "Hello, Sadie? That you?" Another voice, distant at first, said, "Gimme the phone, Jack. . . . Hello."

"Danny?"

"Yeah."

"Still want that money?"

"I don't know what you're talking about." The voice was flat.

"Is this Danny Fuller?"

"Yeah, but take it easy, will you?"

"Oh. I'm sorry. There's no one at this end."

"I couldn't be sure."

"Danny, it's all worked out. We'll get the money tonight. But I've got to know something first. If I help you get it, how do I know you'll give me half?"

"A very interesting question. Next, please?"

"Listen. This is terribly serious to me. How do I know?"

"You don't. But I'll tell you something, gorgeous. You've got about ten times the chance to get a straight deal from me as I have from you—meaning no offense, ma'am."

"You can't mean that!"

"Skip it, honey. What's the layout? You keep me on this phone too long and I'm apt to get nervous."

"You've got to be at McPhearson Park at nine o'clock tonight. Now listen, at the end of the lake opposite the pavilion there's a very dark stretch, and there's a big pine tree there. It's the only pine tree near the edge of the lake; maybe the only one in the park. Do you know a pine tree when you see one?"

"Please. Don't patronize me; I'm sensitive."

"Be there. It's almost in the center of the west shore of the lake. A pine tree. I'll be in one of the motorboats, and I'll come along the shore and signal with a small flashlight. I don't want to have to do it more than once or twice, so be watching!"

"Will you have the dough with you?"

"Yes. of course."

"Then what's the idea of all the complications?"

"Do you wear a topcoat?"

"I don't own one."

"All right. Remember this: we won't get another

chance. You've got to be there." Jane didn't hear his answer. Someone knocked lightly at the door. The knob turned. The knock came again, a little louder, and Jane said quietly into the phone, "What?"

"I asked you a question. Why all the fuss? Why a boat? Why can't you just meet me somewhere? And what's wearing a topcoat got to do with it?"

Her hand was wet and the phone kept slipping around so she had to hold it with both hands. "It's my husband," she said quietly. "If it weren't for him, the thing would be simple. But we've got to do it this way. When it's over I'm . . . leaving him."

"I'm fascinated," he said cheerily. "I don't like your setup, beautiful. It looks like a snipe hunt. I don't like it at all. Try me again sometime."

For a panicked moment she thought he had hung up. She screamed, "Danny!"

"I'm still here."

"Listen!" She had been standing. She stumbled over to the chesterfield, kicking the cord away from the stand, and sat down. "It's not a trap or whatever you're thinking. I had to pick a place where I knew . . . you couldn't do anything but play fair with me. You know it isn't a trick!"

She could hear him breathing into the phone. "It's too screwy to be a trick," he said. "If you were setting traps for me, it would mean someone was in it with you. They wouldn't rig up something like this. This could only be your idea, gorgeous. I'll be there. Opposite the pavilion, under the pine tree, McPhearson Park, nine o'clock tonight." He hung up.

Jane sat holding the dead phone and staring at

the door, trying to see behind it, to see if Kathy was still there. She stood up shakily and put the phone back on its cradle and went to the door.

She hesitated a moment, then unlocked the door and opened it wide. Kathy was at her own door. She looked up and Jane asked her to come in. She came down the hall, putting her key in her purse, and went on in and sat down.

"Why don't you ask me," Jane purred, "why the door was locked?"

Kathy looked up, and Jane thought angrily that one never knew whether the girl was anxious or confused. Her expression always. perhaps deceptively, implied a little of both.

Kathy said, "It didn't occur to me, Jane. It's certainly none of my business."

"That's awfully virtuous, darling. But I don't want you getting any mistaken impressions."

"I'm not making a virtue of it," Kathy said quietly. "If I got any impressions. I've already forgotten them. Can't we just leave it at that, Jane? I want you and Alan to . . . stay together, Jane. Always remember that."

"Do you think we're planning to separate?"

"No! What's *with* you today, anyway?"

Jane sat down. She was tight inside, and sick. She had to know. When it was all over, there must be nothing, not even a name. And she knew that Kathy had heard a name. "I suppose you heard me on the phone."

"I suppose I did. I heard you say 'Benny' or something. But it meant nothing to me, Jane. I don't enjoy gossip, even if I thought I had something to gossip about."

Jane looked at her hands and whispered. "I did say 'Benny.' He's someone I—"

Kathy stood up quickly. She was frowning now. "Please. Jane. Don't tell me anything. You don't have to."

Jane smiled. "All right. It's all over anyway, and it never really got started. I'm sorry I snapped at you."

Kathy looked relieved, and they talked for a while about nothing at all. Ten minutes later Alan was home and Kathy was leaving.

When they were alone, Jane kissed him and smiled brightly and said, "Darling, take me out to dinner. Just the two of us."

"Again? Hey, take it easy."

She said, "Tonight's special, lover. Please. We'll have dinner somewhere not too expensive, and then go to the park again, like we did the other night."

He grinned. "All right, Jane. Out it is. What's so special about tonight?"

"I laid out some clean underthings and a shirt. And wear your dark suit. I like you best in that. It's not really special. I just said that."

He shook his head at her, kissed her and went into the bedroom, and pretty soon she could hear the shower running. She opened the closet door, looked back toward the bedroom and listened. She stooped down and felt at the hem of the coat. The ticket had worked its way into the corner at the left front hem, crisp and square. She left it and straightened up and went into the kitchen to mix some drinks,

She was in the living room, pouring the drinks

from the frosted silver shaker. She could see Alan putting on the shirt she had laid out for him.

She said, "There's a Martini in here for you." He answered that that was just what the doctor ordered, and pulled a maroon tie off the rack and began to tie it. The coat of the dark suit was lying on the bed. Jane saw him turn to the coat and pick it up. He moved to put it on, then held it out and looked at the lining.

"That's funny," he said. "The label's been taken out of the coat."

"Ye-es," Jane breathed. "I noticed that when it came back from the cleaner's."

He put the coat on and came in and picked up his Martini. "Nice. Just right, Janie." He winked at her.

She breathed again and said, "Yes, I made it with dry sherry instead of vermouth. Don't you think it's better that way?"

"Much. Where's your coat?"

"You go ahead. I'll put it on." She turned abruptly and walked into the bedroom, trying hard to keep from running, wondering what to do if he followed. She couldn't let him help her with the coat. He'd feel the weight of the gun. And she had to get her handbag. In the bedroom she turned and looked back. Alan had gone to the hall closet. Her heart was pounding. It was a small thing, but she had overlooked it! She hurried into the coat and brought the handbag out of the drawer, lifted it up and put it carefully under her arm, and walked out to the door. Alan was putting on the topcoat. It wasn't a new coat. It was something he had had before the war, a dark blue material with a lighter blue check running through it. It was a college boy's coat, the kind of coat people would notice.

She said, "Sweetheart, you looked so nice the other night wearing a hat. Wear it tonight, will you?"

He glanced at her sharply and said, "You're not serious?"

"But I am. Please, do it for me."

The look was puzzled now. He said, "What's up, Janie?"

"How do you mean, Alan?"

"I don't know. That peculiar call I got at the bank yesterday. You and the excursion to the lake. And now a hat! You wouldn't be throwing some kind of a surprise party or something, would you?" He grinned.

"It's just that you've grown up, darling. You don't look dressed without a hat, and tonight I feel festive."

"If it makes you happy, bring on your damned hat."

They went to Pasquale's for dinner. It was a small, one-room place on Melrose, but not an inexpensive place to eat. It was crowded and they had to wait for a while. It was something Jane hadn't planned, having to stand in a crowded restaurant. She stood stiffly, seeing nothing, the whole world a gun in her pocket and a handbag that weighed a ton. It was warm in the place, and she knew that Alan was going to tell her to take off her coat. He was going to want to hold it for her, and she was going to have to keep him from doing it.

Alan turned to her and said, "Janie, you look pale. Anything wrong?"

"I'm all right."

"They ought to turn on some heat in here."

"Wh-what, Alan?"

"It's cold in here."

"I didn't notice."

The headwaiter came and led them to a booth. When they reached it, the handbag under her arm was suddenly an alien thing. What did one do with a handbag? Hold it on one's lap? Put it on the table? Or on the bench, out of sight? She sat down and laid it beside her gingerly and dropped the coat from her shoulders. The waiter was taking their order and Alan was suggesting something to her. She didn't hear him. But everything was all right again.

She nodded and said, "That would be fine."

They left Pasquale's at seven-thirty. She had had to fight off the supplications of the waiter and Alan's bantering to keep from eating a dessert. Pasquale's pastries were the specialty of the house. But Jane wasn't eating dessert. It was important. At five minutes after eight they were in the pavilion at McPhearson Park, and Jane was telling Alan that she was sorry now she hadn't eaten a dessert, she was hungry again.

So they had two hot-fudge sundaes served by the girl with the apple cheeks. Jane talked with her, and the girl remembered them and asked if they expected to be steady customers.

Alan said they might, and the girl smiled and said, "You two don't fit. In the daytime we have married people with kids, and at night we have the kids." She grinned and added, "Grown up a little, of course."

Then they were down on the landing and Alan was talking to the boy in the basque shirt and they were waiting. It would be longer this time, possibly twenty minutes. That was because Jane had insisted on having one of the big boats. "I want to stretch my legs. I was cramped last time." The handbag was a monstrous thing that grew heavier with every moment, and her arm and shoulder were numb and the muscles along her left side burned. Alan was talking too much to the boy. The boy liked to talk, and he liked Alan. She could see that. He would be waiting for them to come back. "Alan, come and look at the ducks."

The boy jumped forward and guided one of the large boats alongside. Two girls with sloppy sweaters and two boys with dull eyes and stains on their mouths stepped out.

The boy in the basque shirt nodded to Jane. "It's yours," he said.

Jane sat at the stern while Alan guided the boat out toward the dark center of the lake. She had put the bag down beside her and the gun was heavy on her thigh. She wanted to rub her arm and shoulder, but she couldn't. In the center of the lake, Alan shut off the quiet motor and turned and grinned at her. She could see the whiteness of his teeth and the soft red lights from the shore dancing in his eyes. He took off the hat and tossed it onto the seat beside her. She saw him look off to the left where the lights of other boats moved dimly. The sound of the mallards was quiet and sleepy.

Jane glanced at her watch. Thirty minutes. There was infinite relief in that. Thirty long minutes of respite. She looked up at Alan again, and he was still lost in the things seen dimly across the lake. And as she watched him, slowly something gave way within her and she found that there was no drive, no clarity, no conviction, no cold rod of resolve to sustain her. She knew abruptly that she could not kill Alan. She had known it all along. These last few days had been a hoax played upon herself, an elaborate subterfuge, an escape, to put off for as long as possible the need to face that which she could not face: the loss of the round bright future, the return to Burbank or to the dark river lapping with cold tongue at the piers of Tulsa. She could not kill Alan.

"You're so quiet tonight, Jane." He was smiling. He raised a hand and put it inside his coat. He brought it out and patted the topcoat pockets and said, "Damn. Left my cigarettes up there." He leaned forward. It was too late. There was nothing she could do. He reached out and took hold of the handbag, and his hand came up an inch and stopped. The hand pulled, and the bag moved sluggishly, and from it came the soft sound of heavy metal falling against metal.

Alan looked up slowly. "What's in your purse?"

"Nothing." Her voice was as dry as pulp. "It must be caught on something. There—there aren't any cigarettes in it."

He moved closer and opened it and put in a hand. He brought it out again empty, and he didn't move. He was half kneeling, half sitting, staring down at the dark bag as if there were something unfolding there from which he could not look away. And then he slowly raised his head, and his eyes looked into hers and held them. The eyes were inside her, opening dark doors within her and beyond her, and the things behind the doors were things she had never seen and could never see. She felt the weight of the gun in her hand, and she brought it down out of the dark, heavy with agony and terror; brought it down again and again; even when she knew it no longer carried the thing with which it had begun.

Alan was dead. There was blood. Blood on her right hand and blood on the gun and on the sleeve of her coat, and a black and gleaming stain of blood where Alan's head lay on the bottom of the boat. Jane knew that this was the first moment in a new time. This was the moment of commitment from which time each act was an apogee. She pushed the body away from the blood toward the end of the boat. He moved reluctantly, fighting her now as he had never done in life. She took the little flashlight from her pocket and put the light on Alan's coat. No blood on the coat. No blood on the sides of the boat. She put the light back and raised herself and put her hand up under her dress. She unhooked her half-slip and let it fall. She put it over the side until it was wet through, and cleaned her hand and sleeve and the gun and the floor of the boat.

She looked at her watch. Ten minutes till nine. She wet the slip and scrubbed the floor of the boat again. She rinsed the slip out in the water and rung it out and rolled it into a tight ball and pushed it into the pocket of her coat. Alan was dead.

The boat had drifted toward the west end of the lake, and a small boat was moving toward her, going nowhere. Traffic on the boulevard rolled by in distant silence. Jane pulled the switch, and the boat began to move slowly toward the shore. She could see the pine tree, tall in the moonlight, and the thick darkness beneath it. She swung around and came down slowly, close to the shore. When the boat was several yards from the tree, she looked at her watch. One minute after nine. She threw off the switch, and the boat slowed and the water lapped silently against it as the boat drifted. She turned it closer to the bank, only inches away, and pointed the flashlight toward the darkness under the pine and let the light beam out briefly, twice.

She waited. No shadows moved, nothing stirred in the darkness under the tree. She flashed the light again, swinging it in an arc. No one came. She tried it again. She waited five minutes, then ten. No one came.

It was only an aura of terror at first, bright and cold and without form. She pushed the switch blindly and guided the boat away from shore. She thought of nothing. A small boat went by and someone laughed as it turned sharply and sent waves rocking against the boat.

She sat in the bobbing darkness and slowly let the thought sicken through her. Danny had changed his mind. He hadn't come and he wasn't coming. She stared down at Alan's dark and huddled body. The boat rocked gently, seeming to move, and moving nowhere. Another boat glided by off to the right, and the sound of music danced sweetly across the water.

PART THREE

NO more than Alan, did Jane move or think or feel. She was waiting, giving no thought to what she would do, because she did not accept the necessity of it. Danny would come. She raised her arm to look at her watch, and put her arm down again. Minutes later she realized she hadn't looked at the watch. She raised her arm again. It was nine-thirty-five. She looked off in the direction of the pine. The darkness under it was as cold and comfortless as the tomb. Slowly and without conviction, she pulled the switch and started back toward the tree.

She came in close to the bank and turned on the flashlight and left it on and swung it in a wide arc. Something moved. A part of the shadow separated itself from the darkness and moved toward her and became a man. Danny Fuller was stepping into the boat. Jane was at the wheel, Alan's body beside her. Danny stumbled and sat down on the cushion in the stern, and Jane threw the switch and turned the boat toward the center of the lake.

She loved Danny. She wanted to throw her arms about him and tell him so, to tell him that he was joy and humor and the breath of life!

She said, "Where were you?"

"I don't just walk into things, beautiful. I had to check on— What's that?"

"My husband. He's dead. Don't move, Danny; I have a gun pointed at your stomach."

Danny Fuller gasped.

"It's all right. I'm not going to kill you. You're going to help me."

"Like hell I am! Listen. I don't want the money any more. Do you take me back to shore or do I swim?"

"If you move, I'll shoot you. Then I'll tell them you killed my husband. Perhaps that's the best way to do it."

Danny Fuller said nothing at all. Jane flashed the light on him and saw that he was sitting stiffly with his hands at his aides. She said, "Pull your coat aside. . . . Now the other side. . . That's fine. Now the pockets. . . . Good. You don't carry a gun, Danny?"

"I wouldn't know how to use it."

"I want you to know something. I need you. Not only now but later, when we have the money."

"If you want my help, let me off this scow."

"Stop it, Danny. You haven't anything to worry about. I need you. And no one is ever going to know about this. I've worked it out to the last detail. My husband and I took this boat out a little more than an hour ago. He and I will get off again in just a few minutes. You'll be wearing his coat and hat. I'll pay for the boat and you'll go on up the stairs and out to the car. My husband won't disappear until some time later. Are you going to help?"

"Have I got a choice?"

"No."

"I'll help."

"You'll never have a choice, Danny. If anything ever happens because of you, I'll swear you were in it from the start. Do you think they'll believe you or me?"

"Don't rub it in."

She helped him take the blue topcoat from Alan's stiffening body and watched him put it on. She threw the hat to him and told him not to turn the brim down in back. He put it on.

"What do we do with that?"

She lifted the handbag over to him and told him what he would find in it, and gave him instructions. But she didn't help. She had him remove the things from Alan's pockets and put them in the bag, then he tied the weights and the fish line around the legs and arms. Jane took the boat to the center of the lake and waited until the other boats were a long way off. Then they picked Alan's body up and lifted it over the side and lowered it slowly. The dark water closed round it silently.

She had Danny scrub the boat again and she gave him more instructions, telling him what to do if a dozen things, that would never happen, occurred. She warned him that Alan had left his cigarettes somewhere, perhaps at the fountain in the pavilion, and that he should keep to the right going through the pavilion and not hear it if anyone called to him.

Then they took the boat in. Jane got out first, smiled at the boy in the basque shirt and said, "I have something for you.

His eyes bugged slightly and stayed on Jane's face. He said, "Yeah?"

Jane gave him a dollar and said, "That's for getting us a boat so soon."

Danny had gone on up the stairs now. Jane paid for the boat and hurried after him. The girl at the fountain was busy, but she looked up and saw

Jane looking at her and nodded. Jane smiled at her and went on out. Danny was at the wheel. They put the top up and drove to the Chateau Michel.

DANNY eased the nose of the car down the ramp slowly, ready to put the car in reverse and back out if Pete was too near the entrance. But Pete wasn't in sight, and Danny pulled into the Palmer parking space and Jane jumped out. She walked down the long line of cars until she found Pete waxing an ancient black sedan. She called to him from the center of the aisle, so that he would have to come out where he would see the convertible with a man at the wheel and the sleeve of the familiar coat resting along the door. She said Mr. Palmer wanted to get the car waxed tonight if possible.

"Sure thing, Mrs. Palmer."

"Fine." She turned and nodded. That was Danny's signal to back the car out. She called out, "Oh, Alan! Get some cigarettes while you're there! The sleeved arm waved and the car backed up the ramp and disappeared. She smiled at Pete and said, "He's going down and see if he can talk the corner drugstore out of some after-hours whisky."

Pete allowed that it probably wouldn't be too hard to do. He excused himself and went back to work on the black sedan. Jane walked back down and took the elevator to the seventh floor. She knocked lightly at Kathy's door.

The door opened and Kathy stood there looking very small and very sleepy.

Jane laughed. "Did I get you up?"

"No," she smiled. "I was reading on the couch. Guess I dozed."

Jane went in and sat down and said, "Alan's gone down to the corner to get a quart. Will you have a nightcap with us?"

Kathy was touched. "Fine idea. Frankly, I was afraid you were miffed with me."

"Don't be silly."

They sat, talking around the silences like people having difficulty keeping their footing on a hard climb.

Jane was watching the time. In twelve minutes she said, "Wonder what's keeping him?"

"It's after hours, Jane. He's probably having a little trouble talking them into it."

"I suppose that's it." She waited six minutes more and said, "Kathy, will you call the garage and ask Pete if he's seen Alan?"

Kathy nodded, and Jane felt a sudden warmth of confidence and achievement. Having Kathy call was an added touch, a creative act that lifted and strengthened her.

Kathy came back and said, "Pete says he hasn't seen him since he came in with you." Jane looked down at the floor, trying to let the feeling of triumph die, so she could carry on with what she had to do.

She stood up and said, " I'm going to see if he's in our apartment. I told him I'd be here with you."

In her apartment, Jane locked the door. That wouldn't look good if Kathy came down, but it would look worse if Kathy found her putting the gun back and taking Alan's wallet, pen and miscellaneous notes from her bag.

Kathy was making coffee when Jane came back. "He isn't there."

"Don't worry about it. Why don't you call the drugstore?"

Jane did that. The man at the drugstore said Mr. Palmer hadn't been in at all that evening. Jane felt a moment of genuine surprise, then she laughed inwardly and thought, *That's the thing, believe it. Alan isn't lying in the mud of a cold lake. He's gone somewhere. He told me he was going after liquor, and it was a lie. He didn't go. He has left me.*

There was consternation and surprise and incipient anger in her face when she turned to Kathy and said, " He didn't go to the drugstore at all."

"Don't worry about it, Jane. He hasn't been gone a half hour yet. I'm making you some coffee."

They sat and drank coffee, and the silence lengthened and became eloquent. Jane told herself that Kathy was accepting Alan's disappearance, that she was attributing it to Alan's having found out about the man she had heard Jane talking to on the phone.

Jane stood up and said, "What should I do?"

"You should go to bed and forget about it until you know something's really happened. I'll go help you."

That was fine. Jane would have asked her to come if Kathy hadn't volunteered. Jane needed a witness to her going to bed. She would keep Kathy there for an hour or two and then send her home. Jane undressed and Kathy helped by hanging up her things.

Slipping into her negligee, Jane said, "Don't leave, Kathy. I couldn't sleep. Stay for a little while, will you?"

"Of course."

Jane picked up the phone and carried it to the chesterfield and sat down with her feet tucked under her. "I keep thinking he'll call."

Kathy nodded. They talked about Alan then, and Jane found that she could talk about him and remember him and feel a warm sorrow. But it touched her only faintly and a little sadly and without remorse.

Almost an hour passed. Jane lifted the receiver and dialed the operator. She asked to be connected with police headquarters. She heard the whir of the phone at the other end, a girl answered, and Jane said, "My husband is missing and I—"

"One moment, please."

The distant whir and a man's voice saying, "Business office."

"I want to get help to find my husband. He—"

"Lady, the Missing Persons Detail closes at five P.M."

"But . . . you mean that you can't do anything tonight?"

"How long's he been missing?"

"Almost two hours. He was just going up to the corner."

"Lady, there's nothing we can do tonight except take your report. You come down here tomorrow and make a report in person—if he hasn't shown up yet—and we'll go to work on it."

"Then you won't even check on accidents or anything tonight?"

"We just haven't got the staff for it, Mrs. — What is your name? I'll be glad to take a report."

So Jane made her report and hung up and forced herself to think bitter thoughts about the

Los Angeles police because Kathy was watching her.

She told Kathy what had been said, and Kathy shook her head and asked, "Can I fix you something to drink, Jane?"

Jane nodded, looking sad. Kathy stood up and went into the kitchen. And Jane's stomach suddenly pulled up into a tight and sickening knot, and she leaped up and stood with her fist to her mouth, wanting to scream at Kathy to come back, wanting to wave her arm and wipe Katherine Palmer away. But it was too late. It was a little thing again, just a tiny thing that she had given no thought to. But it was an error, and it could kill—

She sat down again, cold and shaken, hearing the dainty sound of ice cubes dropped into glasses. She could see Kathy now, opening the cupboard and seeing the bottles there. There was everything there, the best. It had been one of the things Jane had spent the money on that Alan had complained of. Stocking their larder. She heard the sound of the siphon, then the rhythmic tinkle as Kathy carried the two glasses into the room.

Jane forced herself to look up, and to keep the terror from her eyes. Kathy was biting her lower lip with the earnestness of her effort to keep from spilling the drinks balanced on a tiny tray. Jane took one of the glasses, and the tray tipped up a little and some of Kathy's spilled. Kathy laughed. So she hadn't noticed. Sweet, kind, thoughtful, innocent Kathy hadn't thought of it yet. But she would. She would. Oh, just give her time!

Jane tasted the drink, and it was flat and without warmth. Kathy sipped at hers and talked about things that could have happened to Alan that were not at all serious. Jane put her half-finished drink aside behind the lamp, out of the way. Why didn't Kathy finish hers? Why did she sit there sipping at it, holding it up in front of her face like a simpering schoolgirl'? Why didn't she drink it, get it out of the way, forget it?

It was a long time before Kathy finished. And Jane hadn't thought of what she would say when it finally got through to Kathy that she had mixed two highballs out of good bonded bourbon.

Kathy stood up and said, "Where's your glass?"

"Oh, right here. I guess I didn't finish it. I don't care for another."

Jane took the glass out from behind the lamp and handed it to Kathy. The girl gave her a puzzled look and stepped over to take it. She froze, her hand outstretched. It dropped slowly to her side, and she stood staring down at Jane. Jane was fighting the terror that was rising in her, telling herself that it didn't prove anything, that she was stronger than Kathy. She looked up and met Kathy's dark eyes, that were round and full of doubt and slow fear.

Kathy's voice was high and small and pinched. "Why should Alan have gone for a bottle of something? You have everything in there—everything!"

It was Jane who looked away. "You're right," she whispered, and put a note of wonder in her voice. "It means he never intended to go to the drugstore."

Kathy sat down slowly and waited until Jane looked at her again. She said. "Where's Alan, Jane?"

"What do you mean by that?"

"Are you trying to tell me that both of you forgot you had a cupboard full of liquor?"

"I'm not trying to tell you anything. Why should I? Alan told me he was going after a bottle. It just didn't occur to me that we didn't need it!"

Kathy said nothing.

"What did you mean by asking me 'Where's Alan?' "

"I don't know, Jane. I'm sorry. I got excited."

Jane stood up. "I'm going to bed. I know nothing's happened to him now."

"Yes."

They said their good nights and Kathy was gone. Jane stood and glared at the door. Kathy. What was she thinking? What could she possibly suspect? Forget it. Kathy was the kind the world turned out by the millions, like things turned out on a machine, the female equivalent of Alan, conforming, cowardly, without strength. Jane remembered that yesterday she had cried. She had cried because she believed that she was going to kill Alan. And she had killed him, irrationally, in terror, out of the idiocy of accident. But the thing she had done had given her a renewed strength, a renewed awareness. She had rediscovered herself, and she knew that she would never cry again.

SHE dressed in the darkest clothes she could find, put the things from Alan's pockets into a paper sack and the service automatic into her handbag. She pulled on gloves, turned off the lights and listened carefully at the door. She opened it quietly, stepped out and walked down the six flights of stairs and out by the side entrance. She walked rapidly up Farrel to the place where she had told Danny to take the car. She knew Danny would be there, because Danny wanted his money. And she knew that he wanted all of it.

The car was there, tucked in neatly between the board and the building. But Danny wasn't in it. She slid under the wheel to wait. It didn't worry her. Danny was being cautious again. He would be around. Fifteen minutes later, the door opened and Danny was standing there with a hand in the pocket of Alan's coat, pushing it out at her. There was something else in the pocket too. That was what he was pointing at her through the cloth.

He said, "All right, tiger, give me that canister you were waving around down at the lake."

"Canister?"

"The gun; and I'll take it butt first."

Jane laughed lightly. "Danny, you haven't got a gun in that pocket, and I haven't got a gun with me to give you. So stop being silly and kiss me."

"First I'll have the gun."

"I don't have one. Do you want me to get out and let you search me?"

"That might be fun."

"Except that we have a lot to do tonight if you want that money. I can't take a chance on being gone too long."

Danny pondered that. Then he grinned and took his hand out of his pocket. There was a bent stick of wood in the hand. He looked at it wryly and said, "Can't do much with this, anyway." He threw it away and got into the car. He pulled Jane against him and she let his lips have their way with her for a while, then she pushed him away and said, “Danny, wait. We’ve got a lifetime ahead of us. But right now every minute counts.”

He let go of her slowly. “I didn’t know they made ’em as beautiful as you, tiger,” he said huskily. “I didn’t know they made ’em as hard as you either.”

Jane wasn’t listening to what he said. She backed the car out, dropped down to Sunset by a side street and turned west. She drove slowly, stopping clean for all signals, slowing almost to a stop for the yellow lights. By the time they reached Bel-Air, it was well after midnight and the traffic had dropped away to nothing.

Danny said, “Don’t tell me you buried the dough.”

“What else?”

“Almost anything else.”

“You’ve never told me, Danny, how you happened to know we had the money.”

“I didn’t know for sure. I knew I didn’t get it. I was in the car that followed you down the hill.”

“Where did it— I mean, how did it happen that way?”

“I’ll tell you that when I see the dough.”

At Belagio Road she swung right and started up the grade into the hills. There were great, shrub-hidden houses along here set about two hundred feet apart, but as the road climbed higher they became fewer, and then there was a mile of twisting road cut out of the hillside, with a sheer drop to the right, and here there were no houses at all. The car picked up speed.

Danny had fallen quiet and Jane could feel him begin to stiffen. Silently the tension grew inside the car, and Jane knew that she must think of something to dispel it, to get Danny relaxed and off his guard. She glanced at him and smiled, but he didn't see it. He was staring out at the dark road, his jaw set, a few tiny beads of sweat standing on his brow.

The road turned back on itself and leveled out, and below them in the distance stretched the long straight prongs of light that marked Wilshire and the other boulevards that forked out from the city toward the sea. Here there were more houses, smaller, set down from the road with their backs turned to it aloofly. The road turned sharply again and a big sleek car loomed up broadside before them. Jane drove her foot against the brake and the car lurched upward, tires screaming, and jolted to a stop. The big car was pulling out of one of the driveways, and it was almost facing them now.

There was a sudden movement beside her, and Jane turned and saw Danny Fuller going out.

He slammed the door and turned and shouted, "Not this time, tiger! Not Danny Fuller! I'll see you sometime when there's daylight, and a million people around! And I'll get my dough! Don't worry about that!"

He was off down the road, running fast, and the big car's lights were on him and on her. There was nothing she could do. The car roared by, lighting the way in the direction Danny had gone. But she knew Danny hadn't stayed on the road. There was no use turning, no use searching. He was gone.

She sat and looked out across the long hood at the blue infinity of sky and let her mind turn slowly. And she knew that she felt only warm relief. Let him go. She had thought it necessary that Danny should die. And now she wondered at herself and was appalled. There was no menace in him. He would never tell. He would make no move against her until he knew where the money was. And before he knew that., she would be gone from here. She would be in Mexico. She shook her golden head slowly, and she almost smiled. She doubted that she could have killed Danny anyway. Let him go.

And then quite suddenly the whole dark vault of the night closed in on her and smothered her, an emetic that sickened through her and twisted her as hands tore at the key and feet jabbed wildly to start the car, to make it move, to carry her out of there, back down the road. To find Danny Fuller, who was wearing a dark blue topcoat, who carried in the lining of that coat the key to a dream.

TWO hours later Jane gave up. She had no choice. There were things to be done. She drove down to Pacific Palisades and turned onto Chautauqua, which dropped abruptly down onto the highway. The ocean was rough and noisy and menacing. Jane drove along beside it, feeling the bitter cold of it and yet being quieted by it. Its dark and lonely bulk belittled her and her problem. And she drew strength from it, and hope. There was a chance that Danny would do nothing with the coat just yet. He wouldn't just throw it away, because he was involved in Alan's death. He would want to be rid of it safely. That might take time. And Jane had the number he had given her. She would find him. She would give Danny half the money, if necessary.

She would find him.

She found a place where the road widened and there was deep shadow from a two-story building, dark and deserted. About two hundred yards down, stairs went up the cliff onto the boulevard, where she would be able to find a cab. This was it. She stopped and took the paper bag from her pocket. The pen she kept. She could simply leave that in another of his suits. The papers she put in the glove compartment. The wallet she took in her hand and left the car. She walked down to the beach as far as the shadow of the building would let her. She threw the wallet and saw it drop into the churning breakers. Perhaps it would wash up again later, perhaps not. It didn't matter.

It was five A.M. when she walked back into the Chateau Michel. She used the same door she had used earlier, and no one saw her. She walked up the stairs. She was tired. She had had the taxi let her off ten blocks away. At her own floor she walked quietly and quickly to her door and unlocked it. As she was going in, she heard a door down the hall being unlocked. She went in hurriedly, closing the door quietly and turning the bolt. She ran to the bedroom. She didn't know, but the other door could have been Kathy's. She began to tear off the clothes and throw them under the bed.

The knock came lightly, timidly. Jane finished undressing and got into the nightgown she had been wearing when Kathy left. The knock came again. Jane mussed up her hair and wiped off her lipstick. The knock came again, louder.

Jane opened the door and Kathy came in, a blue robe wrapped around her. Jane turned on the light, and Kathy looked around the room expectantly.

She said, “Alan came in, didn’t he?”

“Why, no.”

“But I heard the door open.”

Jane glanced about the room. “But you couldn’t have.”

Kathy’s face suddenly lost all trace of expression. Jane could find nothing in it but dark and neutral eyes that somehow, incongruously, revealed a latent courage. Kathy turned to the door and opened it.

She looked over her shoulder and said, “Your hair is misty, Jane. Better dry it before you go to bed.” She closed the door behind her.

Jane turned off the light and stood in the dark and wondered what Kathy might imagine, what she might do when it became clear that Alan was never coming back. She felt chilled suddenly, and realized that she was standing in the cold room in her bare feet and a nightgown. She went to bed. But she didn’t sleep. And the chill would not go away.

AT eight o’clock the next morning Jane was at police headquarters to make her report in person. At eight-twenty she was in a drugstore phone booth calling the number Danny Fuller had given her. She counted the rings. On the eighth she decided to let it ring four more times and hang up.

On the tenth ring, the circuit suddenly opened and a loose and raucous voice shouted, “Yah? Who ya want?”

Jane put a lilt in her voice and said, “Who am I talking to?”

Nobuddy. This is a pay phone, and I answered it ta shut it up."

"Nobody? You sound like somebody I'd like to know."

"Huh?"

"In fact, your voice is familiar."

"Ya don't say."

"Maybe I should come out and see if you look like you sound. How do you get out there from downtown?"

"Hah! How do I know I wanta see you?" His laughter stabbed at Jane's eardrum, and she jerked the receiver away.

"How do I sound?" she said.

"So-so. How do I sound?"

"Swe-ell-l-l."

"Hah! Hey, my eggs is getting cold!"

"Let's see, that restaurant is on—"

"Beverly and La Brea, babe. Ya comin' out?"

Jane hung up. Beverly and La Brea. She took a streetcar to a used-car lot on Figueroa, where she bought a scarred and unhappy sedan, dark blue in color, and not too noisy. It took a while, checking Jane's account and preparing papers. It was almost ten when Jane arrived at Beverly and La Brea. There was a drugstore on one corner, a drive-in on another and a small white lunchroom on a third. The fourth was a service station. They probably served eggs in the drugstore, so it could be any one of the three places.

She parked and went into the drugstore, got some nickels from a clerk and went into one of the booths. There were three booths. How could she look at all three without attracting attention? The first one wasn't the right number, and she went out immediately, as if there had been something wrong with the phone, and went into the second. That wasn't right either. She stayed in there for a while, then came out and walked around impatiently, like someone being harassed by too many busy signals. Then she went into the third. It wasn't the drugstore.

The drive-in across the street had a phone inside and a booth outside. The number she was looking for wasn't on either phone. That left the white lunchroom. It was called Bill's Beanery. She crossed over to it and went in. It was warm inside and there was an odor of raw-fried potatoes and good coffee. The counter ran the entire length of the place, with about twelve stools. There was a juke box, a cigarette machine and very little else. At the left end, attached to the wall, was a telephone. Jane sat at the left end and ordered fried potatoes and eggs. She was hungry.

The man behind the counter was long and bent, carrying his forty or forty-five years with a weary patience. He brought Jane some coffee in a cup an inch thick, and she sat and waited for it to cool. Four stools up from her there was a short wide man with dark and gleaming skin and a mass of hair like an owl's nest. He wore a dark-blue pinstripe suit and a yellow tie. And he was staring at Jane.

Jane looked up and away again quickly, and she saw the tall man behind the counter shake his head and scowl at the man with the hair.

The man said, "But, Harry, strike me dead if I'm lyin' to ya! It happened!"

Harry wiped the counter and smiled knowingly. Harry was a skeptic. “Okay, George. It happened.”

“So help me. She says, ‘Say, you sound like somebuddy I’d like to know.’ And what a voice, Harry. Then she tells me I’ve really got her going and she wants to know where I am.”

“Then she hung up,” Harry commented.

“Maybe she was anxious.”

“Sure.”

Jane took out a nickel and stepped to the phone. She didn’t really have to look. George had told her all she wanted to know. But she looked anyway. It was the right place. She dialed the number that was on the phone, got a busy signal, hung up and got her nickel back.

Harry brought her the eggs and potatoes. She thought of asking him if he knew Danny. If he did, he might know where Danny lived. But it wasn’t the thing to do. As things were now, there was no connection between her and Danny. She felt she should leave it that way. When she finished, George was still there, glancing anxiously out the window.

Jane drove into the service station across the street from Bill’s Beanery and bought some gas. When the attendant was all through checking things and had taken her money, she said, “Look, this is terribly embarrassing, but my husband has . . . well, disappeared.” Never tell a lie if the truth will do the trick. “He used to go over there to that place a lot, and I’m sort of hoping he’ll show up. I wonder if I could park over there by your air thing. That way I’ll be facing the place and can see him without being conspicuous about it.”

The attendant flushed a deep red and said, "Sure. Sure you can park there. It's okay."

Jane parked. In front of her was a driveway. She could drive out of here and take the car in any direction necessary. Now it was a matter of waiting for Danny to appear. Perhaps he never would, but Jane didn't believe that. He had known the phone number of the place without looking it up. That meant he knew the place well. He probably lived close by and ate his meals there.

At ten-thirty Jane left the car and walked into the station office and called police headquarters. She was connected with the Missing Persons Detail, Sergeant Flanner speaking.

"This is Mrs. Palmer. Is there any news of my husband?"

"One moment, Mrs. Palmer." Distant sounds like echoes in a great barrel, then Sergeant Flanner saying, "One of our men left here to report to you personally, Mrs. Palmer. Isn't he there? Name's Breach."

"I'm not at home right now. I—I was looking in a few places where I thought Mr. Palmer might be."

"Well, Breach has information for you, Mrs. Palmer. He may be waiting there for you."

"What sort of information?"

"I'm afraid I can't tell you that."

"Oh. Well, thank you." She hung up, thinking that it would be all right to stay where she was for a while. Kathy would have gone to work, and all that Breach had to tell her was that their car had been found. But why should they be so mysterious about that? And why in person? She went back to the car. The conversation with Sergeant Flanner kept repeating itself, unwanted, in her mind. At noon, the little eating place across the street filled with customers. She noticed that the clerk from the drugstore ate at Bill's Beanery. The short, wide man with the pin-stripe suit and the yellow tie walked out when the crowd began to gather and wandered down Beverly toward Highland.

By one-thirty the place was almost empty again, and despair was a cold seed within her, and she began to tremble. She told herself to go back. *The man from the police is there waiting, and by now he knows you called and were told that he was there. Don't get them wondering about you. Go back. Now.* But. Jane sat, because freedom and a magic world waited for her too. They were in the coat that Danny would destroy soon, or had destroyed, or had hidden. She couldn't perform a simple act as a part of a larger scheme and then become a slave of the act, lose sight of the goal, abandon the dream. She would wait.

He was wearing the same suit. He stepped out of a car he had driven up onto the hard dirt of the lot behind the lunchroom. It was an old car, with only a remnant of blue paint and a battered grille. He wore no hat or coat. He hurried into the place, and Jane could see him taking a place near the phone. She waited. It seemed an eternity of time. But Danny came out again in twenty minutes and walked back to the car. He backed out onto Beverly, rolled the few feet up to La Brea and turned right, toward Hollywood. Jane had started the car when she saw him stand up. She was behind him now, about half a block. He was driving in the center lane, but not fast. Cars passed them, and after a few blocks two cars filled the space between them. Jane found it easy to follow him. At Eversham he turned left, and Jane speeded up and turned. There was no car in sight. Jane gave an involuntary cry and pushed her foot hard against the accelerator. The next street was Detroit, and to the right in about the center of the block Danny's traffic-racked coupé was parked and Danny was crossing the street. Jane turned and drove up slowly. He took something from his pocket and stepped up onto the walk. Jane increased her speed slightly; Danny had disappeared from view. Then she was alongside his car, and she could see him walking a little tiredly down a broken path between a row of court apartments. They were painted a washed gray down to the windows, and below that was tan stucco with a dark stain rising into it from the ground. There had once been a lawn. He stopped at the third bungalow on the left and opened the door with a key and went in.

Jane drove home. She had to see the man named Breach. And she had to have a gun.

KATHY ran to her, as Jane stepped from the elevator, and took her arm. Kathy's face was drawn, and the warm olive of her skin was faded now and almost gray. She said, "Where have you been, Jane? I've been so worried."

Jane walked on down the carpeted hall and said quietly, "I've been looking for Alan, of course. Why aren't you at work?"

"Work!" A little of Kathy's warm color returned suddenly and she said, "With Alan just . . . swallowed up somewhere? Jane, there's a man here from the police with news, and he wouldn't tell me what it was. I—I'm just—"

Jane stopped and took her arm from Kathy's grasp and said, "He's in your apartment?"

"Yes. He was going to leave. I kept telling him you'd be right back."

"And what else did you keep telling him?

Kathy stared at her in surprise. She said quietly and with slow deliberation, "What is there to tell, Jane?"

"I couldn't say," Jane answered. "I haven't your vivid imagination."

"Jane, this is no time for us to be bickering. Are you coming?"

"No. Bring him into my place, will you?"

Kathy hesitated for a moment and ran down to her apartment, Jane opened her door and left it open, and went on into her bedroom and closed the door. She brushed her hair carefully, bringing a few loosely curling strands casually around onto her shoulders. She freshened her make-up and brushed the dark arch of her brows. Then she opened her door and walked into the living room, where there was a man leaning back on the chesterfield, talking across to Kathy.

He stood, and Jane walked toward him slowly, holding out a timid hand and carrying an air of reserve and dignity. Her sorrows, her manner said, were not for exhibition. She said simply, deliberately avoiding an explanation, "I'm terribly sorry you've had to wait so long. I'm Mrs. Palmer."

And the man did what Jane had expected of him. He looked at her. Not the simple exchange of glances that is a part of social intercourse, but the look that is a sudden, subtle arresting of movement and attention, a fleeting moment of interaction stripped raw of inhibition and amenity. Jane was used to this. She noted another thing. The man's eyes, which seemed to be without lashes, had been hard when he stood up. They were not hard now. Now there was nothing about him that was hard.

He said, with a slow and studied formality, "I'd like to offer the department's sympathies, Mrs. Palmer. I hope we'll be able to help. My credentials." He showed her a sweat-darkened billfold and gave her time to look at it carefully.

Jane said, "Thank you, Mr. Breach. Please sit down."

He sat, and Jane composed herself at the opposite end of the chesterfield and pulled her dress down over her knees. She knew that was the correct approach with Mr. Breach.

The man said, "Your sister-in-law has been very kind to me, Mrs. Palmer, but I'm afraid I can't discuss this in her presence without your permission."

Kathy stood up and said, "Of course. I'm sorry. I'll leave."

Breach glanced inquiringly at Jane, who was looking up at Kathy sweetly and saying nothing. Kathy flushed and turned and went out the door without looking back.

Breach said, "Is there anything you can add to your report of this morning, Mrs. Palmer? Anything at all that might help?"

Jane appeared to think for a moment. "No. I'm sure I told you everything important."

Breach took out a cigar and glanced inquiringly

at Jane. She smiled graciously and nodded. He looked critically at the end of the cigar and said, "We have reason to believe that your husband may have met with . . . foul play." He lit the cigar. Jane said nothing, waiting. "That's why it's important that you tell us the whole story, Mrs. Palmer."

It was like a sudden wrenching away from reality. The man looked so harmless, spoke so softly. But he was playing with her. Her throat was tight now and she knew that she couldn't speak. And there was a burning pressure behind her eyes that made them close involuntarily. When she opened them again, he was still there studying her, and Jane noted irrelevantly that she had been right. They were bald eyes, and they seemed naked and evil. Didn't he ever blink? Why did he stare like that? He couldn't know anything! And time was piling up against her answer. "Foul play?" she whispered.

Breach nodded. "I know it's embarrassing to you, Mrs. Palmer. But if you want our help, we need yours."

The tightness in her throat eased slowly. What was he talking about? "Embarrassing?"

He knocked off a minute grain of ash and almost leered at her. "The other woman," he said.

Confusion pressed in on her, and relief. She knew there had been nothing clandestine in Alan's life. She knew that she was still safe. And the bald-eyed leer of the man made her want to laugh. But she didn't laugh.

She said, "What—what do you know about her?"

"I hate to have to bring it out in the open like

this, Mrs. Palmer,"' Breach droned, "but it's the only thing we've uncovered. A resident of Bel-Air called in this morning about nine o'clock. He's a vice-president of a furniture plant out in Vernon. He was taking some friends home late last night and a car braked to a stop to keep from hitting him as he pulled out of his driveway. He tells us a man jumped out of the car and started running down the road. He thought of stopping to investigate, but the man turned off the road and disappeared into the bushes.

"Well, this Bel-Air man decided the thing wasn't any skin off his nose and he didn't report it—he'd probably had a few. But when he woke up this morning, he thought he'd better call us. He told us the man was wearing a dark topcoat and hat, and that the car was a light-colored new convertible. And"—he knocked some more ash from the cigar—"there was a woman at the wheel."

"Did he . . . say what she looked like?"

"No, he just remembers realizing it was a woman at the wheel. What can you tell us about her?"

"Almost nothing, I'm afraid. I—I've only seen her once or twice. She's shorter than I, hair not so blond, brown eyes, I think. But I don't know where she lives or what her name is!" She put her face in her hands.

Breach nodded sympathetically. "We had a couple men go through the bushes out there," he added. "They didn't turn up anything."

Jane nodded without taking her face from the warm guard of her hands.

Breach said softly, "If there's no more you can

tell me, I'll be getting back to the city hall."

Jane looked up slowly and said, "There's nothing else? The car hasn't been found or anything like that?"

"No, nothing like that, I'm sorry to say."

She stood up and held out her hand, and Breach took it and held it a little longer than he should have. Jane pulled it away from him gently and they went to the door and said good-by again. And then he was gone and Jane was leaning against the door laughing. He had looked so knowing, so brutal, so uncompromising and ruthless. And he was nothing! He hadn't even asked what she had been doing all morning. *Cherchez la femme!* Beat the bushes! Poor Mrs. Palmer. The wife is always the last to know. She went into the bedroom and lay on the bed and laughed warm and delicious laughter; and when the laughter was spent, she stood up and got the service automatic and put it in her handbag. She walked to the door and opened it and looked out. No one there. She walked down to the sixth floor and took the elevator from there.

DANNY FULLER was asleep. He lay stretched in adolescent awkwardness on his day bed in the two-room bungalow on Detroit Street. The afternoon sun lay upon him, and he frowned heavily and perspiration rose on his brow. The heavy frowning and the dampened brow were not the sun's doing or because the air of the room was warm and stale. Danny was dreaming. He was walking among his friends and he was waiting to die. Danny had been bitten by a snake, although the others didn't know this. Danny walked about talking with them and waiting in gripped tension for the moment when he would feel the first sharp pang that would be the beginning of death. He waited to die, but he didn't die. It just hung over him as he moved about in the misty light of the dream.

Danny moved restlessly on the bed, fighting back to reality, where the substance was less unbearable than the dream. He woke up slowly, the tensions still with him, exhausted. He sat up slowly and glared back at the sun. He stood up and went into the bathroom and washed his face and brushed his teeth and shaved. He wondered if a shower would help, and decided it wouldn't. He mixed a drink and picked up his wallet and counted the money in it. Twenty-two dollars.

He sat on the edge of the bed with his drink and rolled bitter thoughts about in his mind. He had always been small time, just a quiet gandy dancer, no truck in corpses, taking small bites from small people. He had had a nice thing doing the spread with Joe in the two-bit card games in the small towns south of L. A. Now Joe had another partner to spread the four-card hands and make them into a nice five-card combination. No, Danny boy had to get up in the world. He was for the big time. And now he was pulling a murder rap and counting pennies. How did he ever get into this anyway?

He wondered if he ought to go up to that tiger's den. He decided not to, and then wondered if it was because he was afraid. No, it was because there might be cops around for a while. He had nothing to worry about. She wouldn't make a move until the heat was off and it was officially totted up as a disappearance. He suddenly grimaced. He was remembering that he still had the coat and the hat to get rid of. How was he going to do that? He couldn't just toss them away. Maybe he could keep them. He needed a topcoat. He shook his head. He decided he was hungry. The sun wasn't so bright now. He wondered what time it was. What was the difference as long as he was hungry? He would go out and eat. Twenty-two bucks.

Danny put on his suit coat and unlocked his door. He locked it again outside and walked down the broken path and across the street to his car. He slid under the wheel and put the key in the ignition lock, but he didn't turn it.

He felt the press of cold steel against the back of his neck, and someone said, "Don't move. And don't do anything silly. I don't intend to kill you. I want to talk to you."

Danny kept his head straight and croaked. "Somehow, gorgeous, I can't believe you. Not that I don't want to."

He felt the muzzle, warm now, leave his neck, and Jane said, "We'll go back inside. I'll be right behind you, so don't do anything stupid."

Danny thought, *I don't have to go inside. She won't shoot me out here, and she might shoot me in there. Then again, she might not shoot me in there, and she might shoot me out here.* Danny said, "All right, we'll go inside."

They walked across the street, Jane carrying the gun gangster-style in her pocket. There was a pine tree growing just a little to the left of where Danny would step up onto the curb. He could dodge behind the tree. Then again, they make coffins of pine. Danny went on down and unlocked his door and swung it wide and walked in. Jane closed the door behind her and switched on the overhead light and pulled down the blind. Danny faced her in the center of the room, his hands stiff at his sides, his stomach a tight cold band. He knew that he was pale, that he was afraid of this blond girl with the beautiful face, and that she knew he was afraid. And he was suddenly ashamed. He stared at the gun Jane had taken from her pocket, and for a brief, hot moment he wanted to force her to use that gun, to fire it into his tight cold stomach and kill him. For the first time he remembered the dream he had had just before he woke up, and the fear of death.

Jane said, " What did you do with the coat—my husband's coat?"

Danny thought about that carefully, and the tightness at the back of his neck began to ease away and his blood to flow again. She wouldn't kill him here. She was worried about the coat. She was picking up loose ends. It was all right.

He grinned slowly. "Do you need a gun to talk about that?"

"I feel better with it."

"With a gun in your hand you're not beautiful."

"Where is the coat?" She said it quietly between clenched teeth.

Danny felt it only vaguely, a mild wonder that worry about the coat could produce the eager tightness in her face, make her feel the need of a gun. He lay down on the daybed casually and put his hands under his head and looked up at her. "Forget it, gorgeous. I took care of the coat."

“How?” The strident urgency in her tone made Danny look at her sharply, but he still couldn’t make anything out of it. She added quietly, “Don’t you see? The coat could undo everything if it turned up in the wrong way.”

“Yeah, I guess it could. But right now I don’t much care. Tell me, tiger, why don’t I get a break? I don’t drink much. I play cards only for a living. Take my word for it, it’s not gambling. But the only girl I ever thought I could love insists on talking to me from behind a gun.”

Jane took a single step and leveled the gun at Danny’s heart. The words choked out. “What did you do with the coat?”

“I can’t help wondering why you don’t worry about the hat. It had his initials in it.”

“Yes, and the hat too,” she said weakly. “What have you done with them?”

“Do you want ’em?”

A muscle tightened across her jaw and her eyes dropped suddenly. “I want to see that they’re disposed of, yes.”

Danny rolled over and sat up. “Okay. I’ll let you get rid of ’em.” He stood up and walked to a closet at the back of the room. There was a shelf a little above eye height, and Danny reached back out of sight along the shelf and pulled. The coat came down in his hand and the hat rolled out onto the floor. He turned and walked toward Jane with the coat in his right hand. He said, “Here, catch.” But he didn’t throw the coat. He brought it around in a swift swipe at the gun and knocked it aside. He closed in and pinned Jane’s arms to her sides and held them tight. “Drop the gun, gorgeous.”

Jane's face was empty and gray, and she dropped the gun. It hit Danny's foot, and he kicked it behind him and pushed Jane away. He stepped over and picked up the automatic and put it in his pocket.

"Now sit down over here." He pointed at the daybed. "Sorry it isn't a little tidier. I didn't know you were going to drop by."

Jane sat down and let her coat fall from her shoulders. She put her golden head against the wall and crossed her legs.

Danny said, "How'd you find me?"

"You had lunch at Bill's Beanery. I followed you away from there. I suppose you can figure out how I found Bill's Beanery."

Danny nodded and the cold sense of fear began to stir again within him. What the hell! Didn't he have the heater in his pocket?

He picked up the coat and said, "Tiger, let us see what there is about this coat." He held it out and studied it casually. He glanced at Jane. There was nothing there to help, unless the hushed stillness and the mannequin face meant something. "Must be important," he muttered. He felt the sleeves, put his hands into the pockets, studied the lining. Then he smiled and said conversationally, "There was a hole in one of the pockets. Let's see if there's anything down there." He turned the coat up and began to feel along the hem. He glanced at Jane again. Her lips looked dry and there was a sickness in her eyes.

He had to go over it a second time before he felt the small square of cardboard in the corner of the hem. He looked up. Jane was studying her left hand as if she were wondering how it had got there. Danny whispered, "Hey, I found it."

Jane looked up, and her face was composed, but Danny saw the tightness in it and knew that it was ready to fly apart like a clay pigeon. He reached down through the pocket and felt for it and got it between two fingers. He brought it up and dropped the coat and held it out before him. He heard Jane draw a quick, rasping breath. She stumbled up from the daybed, and he jumped back, his hand at his pocket where the gun was. But Jane wasn't moving toward him. She stood quite still for a moment staring at the thing in his hand, then she dropped to the floor with a heavy, sickening sound. Danny glanced down at her mildly, then looked back at the piece of cardboard in his hand. It was about two inches square, brown in color, and quite blank on both sides. He put it in his pocket and went into the bathroom

PART FOUR

KATHERINE PALMER fitted the passkey into the lock with a casual air that might have surprised her if she hadn't just come from a greater surprise. She had never thought of herself as an accomplished liar, but to get the key she had told the manager an elaborate and effective story bearing only a slight though imaginative relation to the truth. And even while she had glibly told it, a detached part of her had listened with a kind of admiring horror. But then, she had also never thought of herself as a housebreaker, but she was about to become one. That is, if the key would work. She was pushing it carefully into the lock for a fifth try, and the casual air was becoming something of a strain. She said, "Oh, damn!" and shook the door. The key turned with a smooth and easy insolence.

Kathy was not happy with what she was doing. It was prying, intrusive, everything she had always liked to think that she was not. But she had to decide whether or not to go to the police, and the answer lay in Alan's apartment. Here there would be something to tell her if he had simply gone away—things missing, perhaps even a bag or some of his clothes. But she found that these things were not gone, and she stood by the bedroom window looking out into the hard sunlight while her vague fears rolled into a cold conviction. But she had no affinity for despair, and there was something she hadn't looked for. His service automatic had meant a good deal to Alan. It was the one thing he had kept of all the things that were a part of him through the long war. If he had gone of his own will, he'd have taken it with him. Perhaps nothing else, but he'd have taken his gun.

She knelt at the tall chest and pulled open the bottom drawer. The flannel lay at the back, flat and empty. Her hands flew at the things in the drawer. The gun was gone. She sat back and felt the tensions slowly letting go. She smiled at the realization that she was much less ashamed of what she had done than she was afraid that Jane might come home and find her there. She hurriedly refolded a sweater and put it back where it had been. She drew her hand away, and a finger caught and lifted the newspaper lining the bottom. There was something under the paper. A corner of it had shown fleetingly against the brown wood. She lifted the paper and brought out a small white claim check with the imprint of the Union Passenger Station on it. The stamped date caught her attention and held it. Just one week ago. Her face flushed slowly and she stood up, touched with excitement, yet feeling a vague unease. The so recent date and the careful hiding of the ticket seemed to contradict the testimony of the empty flannel. She dropped the ticket into a pocket and finished straightening the things in the drawer.

She hurried to the door and stood for a moment, listening. The hall was suddenly an alien and hostile place, but time was running out. She caught her breath, gripped the knob and pulled open the door. A tall man in a gray flannel suit was standing in the open door with a lightly closed fist half raised.

He said, "I'll bet you do that with electronics."

Kathy said nothing at all. She had to get out, and the man was blocking her, pinning her there until Jane came home. She thought vaguely of merely pushing him over and going on her way, but he seemed a little large for that. And she had the quick conviction, accompanied by a sinking sensation, that he wasn't selling anything.

"There's no one home," she said weakly.

"That's hard to believe," he grinned.

"Were you looking for . . . anyone in particular?"

"A man named Palmer, but I can hardly remember why."

Kathy smiled halfheartedly up at him and said nothing. The problem wasn't simple any more. He was looking for Alan, which meant he would see Jane eventually and would mention this. Alan would never forgive her for suspecting Jane, let alone checking on her. And, she reminded herself, neither would Jane.

The silence lengthened, and the man suddenly put in, with an almost shy laugh, "Well, as you said, there's nobody home." He took a tentative step backward.

"Oh! I'm sorry. Are you a friend of . . . Mr. Palmer's?"

"We flew together in England. In a weak moment he asked me to drop by if I ever got to Hollywood."

His eyes fell for a moment to something Kathy was holding in her hand. She looked down and dropped it hastily into a pocket. It was the passkey, and when she looked up again, his expression was unchanged. She stepped out and locked the door behind her.

"I'm Alan's sister," she said.

"Then you're Katherine. My name's Blake—Don Blake."

She nodded and said, "I—I live just down the hall." She moved toward her door, telling herself that there ought to be some way out without embarrassing herself and Alan and Jane. Blake walked beside her and they were at Kathy's door and nothing had suggested itself. She opened the door and turned back to Blake. The sound of the elevator doors drawing back broke sharply into her thinking.

She took Blake's arm and cried, "Wouldn't you like to come in?" She stepped back, and Blake stumbled a little on his way over the threshold. Kathy closed the door behind him and stood there while a deep bright flush spread upward from her throat and across her cheeks.

Blake looked at her with a broad and puzzled amity. "Ah, Hollywood," he commented.

Kathy could only shake her head, holding her full red lips tightly closed out of a fear that she would break out crying or laughing; she wasn't quite certain which.

After a while, Blake said, "They're probably gone now. Would you like me to leave?" There was still no gravity in the tone.

"Wha—what?"

"Whoever it was we were avoiding. I think they've gone now."

"Yes," she breathed, "they're gone now."

"Is it anything," he grinned, "where time and a strong back might help? I have a little of both."

Kathy smiled then and shook her head. "I don't think so. But . . . sit down, won't you?" And sitting across from him she said, "It's Alan. He's missing."

"Since when?"

"He drove out of the garage last night about ten o'clock. He hasn't been heard from since."

Blake smiled and seemed to relax visibly. "He's still practicing to be a civilian," he said. "I did that kind of thing for months. You get a sudden impulse to cut loose just to prove that no one's going to come around and tell you how to wear your necktie."

"Thanks, Mr. Blake. You're trying to tell me it's too soon to get upset about it. But it's more than — Oh, I don't know!"

"Have the police been notified?"

"Yes."

"What did you expect to find," he asked quietly, "with your passkey?"

Slowly and helplessly, Kathy reddened again; she could feel the pressure of it behind her eyes.

"I—I suppose I had to expect that."

"Sorry. I guess that was on the officious side. I have ten days coming to me, and I'd looked forward to a stretch of sand where I could go into a happy coma. But I wouldn't like to feel that I walked out on Al. So if there's anything I can do, I hope you'll tell me about it."

She shook her head. "I don't know. I suppose not."

Blake frowned for a brief moment, then took a packet of cigarettes from his pocket and offered her one. She shook her head, and he put one in his mouth and lit it. He held the match, turning it in his fingers until it burned out.

Kathy stood up and brought him a tray, and he dropped the match into it and said, "Where's Mrs. Palmer?"

"I don't know."

"When I meet her, do I mention how I happened to run into you?"

"If you want to be my candidate for the most hateful man living."

"But you were there. It suggests you think the police need some help. Or is it that Jane has them eating out of her hand?"

Kathy looked steadily across at Blake, feeling uncomfortably that she had missed something, that there had been a subtle shift of position and it was Blake who faced a problem. "A few things have happened," she said, "but they're confused, and I don't know what they mean. I'm afraid there's nothing either of us can do."

"But the things that happened concern your sister-in-law. Isn't she the one we were playing hide-and-seek with in the hall?"

The sense of having lost touch with the moment was strong now. The friendliness of the tone, the implicit sympathy, were still there, but now there was a pointed insistence. He was pressing her, questioning her with a curiously accurate insight.

"Yes, it's Jane. But it's nothing; it's only that she may not be telling—" She stopped abruptly, and the silence lengthened and grew heavy, and she began to feel it as a tangible thing. Blake sat smoking easily, glancing at her now and then as if the long silence and what she had said were quite normal things. "I shouldn't have said that," she whispered.

Blake said nothing for a while, then grinned slowly and said, "All right, let's forget it. Where shall I say I met you, in case it ever comes up?"

Kathy leaned forward and raised her hand in an uncertain gesture. The finality of his last words had brought her sharply alert, and she felt suddenly the need for help, the need to tell someone the things she had seen and heard and puzzled over in the last hours.

"Wait," she said. "I'm afraid I'm being stuffy. I keep thinking how guilty I'll feel when Alan comes home for dinner tonight—for being so . . . suspicious, I mean. But I'm afraid I'll feel much worse if he doesn't come home and I haven't done anything about it."

Blake waited quietly, and Kathy made a false start or two and finally got her story told simply and dispassionately. For a reason she did not stop to analyze, she made no mention of the claim check hidden in Alan's drawer. Blake stubbed out his cigarette and stood up, his manner almost diffident now.

"Strange doings," he said, and the tone was light again. "But . . . it's just possible your brother would prefer we stay out of it, Miss Palmer. Or may I call you 'Angel'?"

Kathy rose and said, "Couldn't you compromise?"

"You mean ' Miss Angel'?"

She frowned, and then smiled through it and

said, "My friends call me 'Kathy.' And I agree with you. I want to be a little more certain than I am now before I make any statements to the police."

Blake took a step toward the door and said, "I'd offer my unworthy aid, but I haven't found a place to stay yet. I'll probably have to build."

"Do you mean that about helping?"

"Yes, but—"

"I'll go downstairs with you, Mr. Blake. I think we have a bargain to strike."

JANE was lying on Danny Fuller's day bed watching a fly crawl across the ceiling. Danny was saying, "You all right now? You okay?"

Jane didn't answer. She couldn't rise over the draining sickness within her. She lay and pushed the thought slowly round and round. The way things worked. By their own logic. She knew what had happened. Alan had been afraid to keep the ticket, but he had also been afraid to tell her that he hadn't kept it. It was simple. *Let her think I still have it until the time comes to send it back*. It was so terribly logical, all of a piece. She had had to kill because he had been a coward. And because he was a coward she was defeated, and his death a futile horror without issue. She turned her face to the wall.

Danny said cheerfully, "I'll go turn on the oven. It's cold in here." From the kitchen he said, "Maybe I shouldn't bother to light it, uh, gorgeous?"

Jane turned her head to look at him. It hadn't touched him. Maybe he didn't realize what it meant. He came back and sat beside her and studied her face with a kind of withdrawn compassion.

"So hubby did a cross-up," he whispered. "Is that it?"

Jane sat up slowly and put her feet on the floor. The room spun for a moment and then was still and quiet. She nodded faintly and said nothing.

"The dough is checked somewhere, I gather."

"It was."

"Where?"

"What difference does it make? He sent the ticket to the police or to the district attorney. I forget who he said he would send it to."

"He didn't send it to the police or the D. A. . . . or any other harness shop."

Jane stared at Danny, waiting, afraid to break the spell.

"If he had done that, there'd have been something in the papers. There's no record of that dough, see? And the guy who threw it into your car will never claim it. So there's no reason to play coy about it. If that money had been turned up, the public boys would have been dipping in for some fat rations of publicity. It would make a great story. First-page stuff."

"Maybe they kept it for themselves."

"Unh-uh. They don't know he's dead, gorgeous. Never forget that."

Jane thought about that slowly while warmth began to steal back into her, and courage and hope. She remembered that Alan had said something to the man at the counter. He had hidden the ticket. What had he been planning to do? She shuddered. "I know what the bag looked like and when it was checked. Is it possible to get it without the ticket?"

"Sure it is, tiger. All you got to do is describe

the contents. They check it and find sure enough it's just like we say—full of dough. So they give it to us. Then the cops come and take us away."

Jane got to her feet abruptly. "I've got to get back. The ticket's there someplace. I'm going to find it."

Danny leaned back across the bed. "I'll be watching you, gorgeous. You won't make a move that I don't know about." Jane picked up her bag and ran a comb through her hair and straightened out her face and smoothed her skirt.

She turned to Danny and said, "I have to have the gun. It's got to be put back."

"Sure, tiger," he drawled. "I'll hand your barker back to you. All you gotta do is ask ole Danny and he comes right through." He stood up slowly and faced her. His eyes were round and sad, his head cocked a little to the side. "I'm remembering the ride we took up into the hills last night. Remember, tiger? The money was buried up there. You were taking me up there to give me my half."

He took the gun from his pocket and played with it. Jane's throat was tight, her lips dry. She wet them and tried to find words, but there were none to answer Danny.

"Remember, tiger?" he repeated.

"Yes," she whispered. "I remember."

"You were taking me up to where the money was."

Jane wet her lips again, but she was breathing too fast and through her mouth, and her lips were dry again an instant later.

Danny said, sadly now, "You were taking me up there to kill me, tiger."

" Yes," she whispered.

Danny's mouth stiffened slightly and his lips didn't move when he said, "And now I hand you the gun?"

"Yes. They may look for it. It should be there."

"Yeah." He took a handkerchief from his rear pocket. He put it around the gun and handed it to her, wiping it off as she took it from him. She had the gun now, her finger on the trigger. Danny grinned.

"Don't get me wrong, tiger. I'm not a brave man. But I know you won't kill me. Not right now, that is."

Jane put the gun in her handbag and turned and walked out of there.

THE phone was ringing when she came in. A polite voice said, "This is Mr. Breach, Mrs. Palmer. We have some information for you."

"Yes?"

"We located the car. It was abandoned just outside San Diego. It probably means he went on across the border into Mexico. That makes it tough for us."

Jane couldn't answer. A song was welling up in her, or laughter. Something that made her want to drop the phone and do a pirouette. San Diego! She had left the keys in the car, but she hadn't thought of that. It was obvious, of course. Someone on the highway had found the car there and taken the rest of his trip in comfort.

She said, "Thank you, Mr. Breach. There's nothing else?"

"No. You've heard nothing at all from him?"

"Nothing."

"I see." There was a short silence. Then Mr. Breach said, with a slight tremor in his voice, "You're taking this thing like a real trouper, Mrs. Palmer. We're going to do our best by you."

"Oh, thank you, Mr. Breach. I . . . well, thanks. Good-by."

She hung up and ran into the bedroom and put the gun away carefully and undressed and bathed and dressed again. She made a sandwich and drank some milk. Then she began the search. She started in the kitchen, missing no inch of possible concealment anywhere. It would take a long time to do it this way, but this was the way she would do it. And she would find the ticket.

It was six-forty and Jane was washing her hands at the sink. Someone knocked lightly and the door opened and a voice called, "Jane." Jane went into the living room and told Kathy to come on in and sit down.

Kathy said, "Your face is dirty. What in the world have you been doing?"

"Cleaning up. I have to do something."

"Of course. Has there been any news?"

Jane collapsed on the chesterfield. "Yes," she breathed. "They found the car in San Diego."

Kathy sat down slowly. "San Diego. Then there can't be much doubt that he just went away."

Jane said sharply, "What did you think had happened to him?"

"Why . . . I just didn't think. It just doesn't make sense."

"No, it doesn't make sense. Does anything?"

"Yes. Most things. Jane, did you look to see if

his gun was gone?"

Jane didn't move. It was all right. She could gain time. She was tired. After a moment, she said, " No, why?" And she knew that her voice sounded quite normal.

"Well, I was just thinking that he'd have taken the gun if he knew he was going away. Don't you think he would have?"

Jane turned her head and studied Kathy's tiny face, the color warm beneath the olive skin, the eyes young and large and dark. A face, Jane thought, that would always look vapid and a little puzzled. But was the mind behind it like the face? Why was she talking about the gun? Jane sat up slowly and then stood.

She smiled slightly to cover the coldness in her face and said, "Maybe we should look and see if it's there." She turned toward the bedroom, Kathy following behind.

At the chest of drawers, Jane knelt and pulled open the drawer and turned down a corner of the flannel and revealed the gleam of gray metal. She heard a tiny catch of sound, and looked up to see the brief surprise in Kathy's face,

"What's the matter with you?" Jane was standing now, her face close to Kathy's.

Kathy met Jane's stare and held it. "Nothing," she said. "I just didn't expect it to be there. I was sure he'd have taken his gun."

Through the slow rage that swelled behind her eyes, Jane realized that Kathy had been in the apartment. Kathy, with her winsome child's face. Like coral, pink and lovely, and full of sharp death. It was Kathy all along. The liquor, hearing her come in this morning, and now the gun. Kathy. Jane felt a tight thrill, a coldness like steel, a vague, unformed resolve.

"Someone's at the door, Jane. Jane—"

"What?" Then Jane heard it and smiled an ammonic smile and said, "Let's go see who it is."

"I think I know," Kathy said as they walked from the bedroom toward the door. "It's a man who used to fly with Alan. He came by today, looking for him."

They were at the door now, and the knock came again, still patient and not too loud. Jane gave her blond hair a toss, let her full red mouth turn up a little at the corners, and opened the door.

KATHY had left them alone, and Blake was sitting on the chesterfield across from Jane, telling her that he was sorry to hear about Alan. Jane was listening vaguely and telling herself that coincidences did occur. It was a coincidence and nothing more that a "friend" of Alan's happened by today. She suddenly realized he had asked her a question.

"I'm sorry. I didn't hear you."

"I was wondering if there was anything I could do."

"Thank you, Mr. Blake. The police—I think they're doing the best they can."

"It would be pretty hard to believe that Al just took after some wild geese. He was a great advocate of the home and hearth."

Jane smiled a melancholy smile and said, "Yes, I know. And he had no enemies, certainly. But the car was found today down by the Mexican border." Jane thought Blake's face suddenly became a bit more still, the wide gray eyes even more withdrawn when she mentioned the car.

"Would you like to take a run down there," he said, "in the morning?" Jane looked puzzled.

"We might learn something. You know, poke around and ask a few questions. I've got all the time in the world—I'm a tourist."

"But the police. Can't they do that better than we can?"

"I suppose so—if you stand over them with a bull whip."

"I don't understand."

"I hear police departments are pretty badly undermanned these days. They don't do any more than they have to. But maybe you're right."

"No. I never thought of it like that. I—I think we should go down."

"Let's wait a day or two and see what the police turn up."

Jane nodded, an uneasy tension growing slowly under her skin. It faded in the next instant and left only a vague apprehension. "Are you from out of town, Mr. Blake?"

"Yes. Michigan."

"Where are you staying?"

"Right here. Your sister-in-law used her influence."

"Oh."

Jane realized that the word had come out weakly. The tension was turning into a chill. Don Blake. She had never heard Alan mention anyone named Don Blake. She was sure of it, and Alan had talked of his flying friends a good deal. Too much. Don Blake.

She said, "What did Alan usually call you?"

"Don—when there were ladies present."

She smiled and tried to make the next question sound like an effort at conversation. "How did you happen to run into Kathy?"

"I don't know. I think possibly it was arranged in heaven."

Jane laughed, a bit too unctuously, and rose to go into the kitchen. She smiled over her shoulder and said, "I'm sure you won't refuse a drink."

In the kitchen, she tried to think about the people Alan had talked of most. What were their names? She couldn't remember. But if she heard one, wouldn't it sound familiar? One of Alan's crewmen was here in Los Angeles. He had a service station out on Adams. What was his name? He would know if there had been a Don Blake. She was taking too long with the drinks. What was his name? She finished and put them on a tray and walked back in, smiling, but not too gaily.

She gave him a glass and put a coaster on the arm of the chesterfield. "What squadron were you flying with?"

"Same as Al's, Mrs. Palmer."

Jane tipped her head slightly and said, "Please call me 'Jane'. That is, if you'll allow me to call you 'Don'?"

"All right."

"Where were you stationed in England?"

"Don't you know?"

"Of course. I keep forgetting. Stonehurst, or something like that." The smile was sharp now, but Jane didn't know that. She wasn't thinking about the smile.

"Ipswich."

The man with the service station had been at Ipswich. What was his name? "Ipswich. Of course. I guess Alan was at Stonehurst when he first went over."

"I didn't know we had any operations at Stonehurst."

"Oh, I don't really know. All those English places sound alike, and you never know whether they're cities or little villages or whole counties."

Jane moved her glass in a little circle, so that the ice touched the edges with a relaxed and quiet clinking; and she peered over it at Blake and tried to look as if she felt as relaxed and casual as the soft sound of the ice against the glass. But the man was looking at her, and the look was a challenge. It seemed to say, "I think you're a phony, Mrs. Palmer, and if I look at you long enough, maybe I'll know."

She shrugged it off. Why add to the things she had to worry about? It wasn't that kind of look; it was just boorish and a little hungry, almost a leer, really. She laughed inwardly. After all, he was just another flier; worse yet, an ex-flier. He probably had it all figured out that Alan had left her. That made her a tenpin. It was all so obvious that she began to feel the way she had been trying to appear to feel. She started to smile.

"I seem to worry you, Mrs. Palmer," he said. "I wouldn't want to do that." The smile faded abruptly. It had been a simple statement, but Jane was reading menace and cold cruelty and accusation into it. She had to prove it now. She had to prove that he was just another male, that the offer to go to San Diego was just the first subtle pass, that this last seemingly prodding remark was only a plea for a lead. All right, she would give him his lead and sit back and watch him rise to it. She smiled again, and it was warm because she thought warmth, and she let her eyes grow only the slightest bit lazy, and she said, "You don't worry me, Don. But you're beginning to intrigue me."

"Let's wait till we're sure Al isn't coming back, huh, Mrs. Palmer?"

She sat up stiffly. The remark had come back fast, with an effect that he might have duplicated by throwing his drink in her face. She said, "You made quite a bit out of that, didn't you?"

"I didn't mean to make any more out of it than I found there."

"I'm afraid you did." She stood up. "Drop in again before you leave town. I have to get some sleep now. I'm exhausted."

He rose abruptly and put aside his glass and walked to the door. For a brief moment, Jane had the empty, helpless feeling that he was going to walk on out the door without another word, without looking back.

Then he turned and said, "By the way, shall I take the man with the dark mustache off your back?"

"What . . . did you say?"

"He looks a little pale. I think I can handle him all right."

"But I don't know what you're talking about!"

"All right, but you'd better forget about that sleep. He's lurking around at the dark end of the hall, making like a tenant trying to find his key. I watched him for a while before I knocked. It made him nervous."

"Perhaps he's from the police."

"Sure. They're looking for Al. Maybe they figure the best place to find him is where he lives." He opened the door and went out, closing it softly behind him.

Jane stood in the center of the room, her fists clenched tightly at her sides, feeling a slow pounding in her throat, and forcing herself to forget him, to think of names, an endless meaningless run of names, because she had to remember the name of the boy with the station on Adams. She had to call him and ask him if he had ever heard of a Don Blake. And if he had, to describe him. The door opened quietly and Danny Fuller slipped into the room.

He said, "Excuse me for not knocking, but I don't like the idea of standing in front of your door. Too much traffic."

Jane stared at him and said, "You fool. You were seen out there. For all I know, the man who saw you is a detective."

"But he didn't see me come in here, gorgeous. There are other people on this floor, you know."

"What do you want?"

"Are you kidding? I want my dough, and there are too many exits in this place. I can watch you better from up here. Find the ticket?"

Jane shook her head and went back to the wing chair and sat down. Her head was aching as it had never ached before, hammering steadily and sharply behind her eyes. "Do you intend to live here until I find it?"

"Not a bad idea."

"My sister-in-law walks in here just the way you did."

"Don't take it to heart, tiger. I came up to tell you something. When I've told it, I'll go. And when you've found the ticket, you'll bring it to me. And don't come with any ideas. I got me a gun."

Jane looked at him then, and Danny came over and sat down on the chesterfield and grinned at her. He said, "So if you get that dough and dust with it, it'll be very, very bad."

"I don't intend to."

"That's fine, but let me tell you why it'll be very bad. You want to know about that, don't you?"

Jane said nothing and Danny went on, "I'm gonna take myself down to police headquarters—when you take French leave with the dough, this is—and I'm telling the whole story just like it happened. Once you skip town, they're going to believe me, see? I won't get more than a year or two up at the college. You, tiger, will be found. And you'll be brought back to breathe some of the state's special nonhabit-forming gas."

Jane tried to smile. The muscles in her cheeks quivered a little and gave up. She said, "Don't you think I realize all that? We've got to help each other, Danny, or we'll both be breathing that gas."

"Yeah?"

"Yes. It's my sister-in-law. She's snooped about and stumbled onto things until she knows that something is wrong. It's only a matter of hours before she goes to the police with her story. And she has just enough to—to make them investigate."

Danny's voice was dry, the confidence suddenly

gone. "What has she got?"

"She knows I went out last night after I went to bed. She knows Alan wouldn't have gone after liquor, because we had plenty here. And she knows that Alan's gun was gone for a while and brought back."

Danny licked his lips slowly and stared at the rug.

"You're going to help me again, Danny."

"Yeah?"

"There's no other way out. There are two of us, Danny. We can't stand by and let her kill us! And that's what she'll do."

"How do you keep her from doing it, tiger?"

"She's been upset because of her brother's disappearance. I mean that. She missed work today. She's what the papers will report as 'despondent.' She's going to take poison because of it."

Danny Fuller looked up, questioningly.

"You're going to get the poison."

Danny shook his head.

Jane drew her mouth down tightly across her teeth. "Danny, do you think I want to do it? Do you think I wanted to kill my—to kill Alan? I killed him because he was all the things that were beating me down and driving me to conform and making me betray the good that was in me. Grin, damn you!" Jane stood up and looked down into Danny's eyes and remembered the terror she had felt when Alan's eyes had burned into hers. She wished suddenly that these were Alan's eyes turned up to hers. There would be no terror now. "I killed him," she finished quietly, "so that I could live."

Danny Fuller said nothing.

"You know how to get . . . what I need. I'll do the rest. It's our only chance. We can't put it off. We'll be executed, Danny —"

Danny closed his eyes. "I'll need dough."

"I can give it to you."

He said nothing and his eyes remained closed.

"You'll get it for me tomorrow, won't you?"

Danny Fuller nodded once slowly and whispered, "Yes."

Danny walked down the six flights of stairs, looking back over his shoulder from time to time, and slipped out the side entrance onto the street. The moon was high and bright and a few stars shone dimly. He walked in the shadow of the building up to his car. He didn't see the tall man step out of the shadow and follow. He didn't see him stoop down and run up behind the car after Danny had climbed in and switched on the lights. And he didn't see the man take an envelope from his pocket and write on it. Danny sat stiff and cold at the wheel, seeing nothing. Fear was a damp and palpable presence all about him. He felt a sudden and terrible certainty that his crime was already known. They were dragging the lake. Now. If he went down there— He made a harsh sound in his throat and raised his hands in a stiff and meaningless gesture, then let them drop slowly. He pushed his foot against the starter. He was going down to the Jungle Room for some scat and barrel fever.

KATHY opened the door to Blake's discreet knock, said, "Come in," and gave him what she thought was a sardonic smile. It came out with all the cynicism of the Mona Lisa's. She had spent the past hour contemplating the probability that she no longer had an ally. The thought hadn't occurred to her until she had walked back to her apartment, leaving Blake alone with Jane. She had never quite thought of Jane as a vampire, but she had no mean appreciation of Jane's intuitive genius for finding and exploiting the weaknesses of the male sex. And Blake was a male. He no doubt had his weaknesses. But here he was, and Kathy was nicely restraining any impulse to throw her arms about his neck.

"No visible scars," she commented. "Sit down."

"It was a draw," he said, and walked over to the sofa.

Kathy said, "She's beautiful, isn't she?"

"Uh-huh. Like something you might buy in a swank shop . . . if you could afford it."

Kathy made no comment on that. She considered how, a few days ago, she would have resented it.

And then Blake added quietly, "I'm afraid Alan couldn't afford it."

Kathy sat down across from him. It was very still in the room, and from below them came the sound of a window being opened for the night. "Why do you say that?"

"Her conscience. It's very, very heavy. She thinks I'm anyone but who I say I am. And she had a caller after I left, a tacky character who carries a gun in his pocket . . . unless it's a pipe wrench."

"But what could it mean? Why would Jane—"

"I don't know, Kathy. But it's time to call the constabulary."

"That department, or whatever it is, closes at five."

"It would. What did they do last night? Do you know?"

"Jane told me they went to Pasquale's for dinner, then down to McPhearson Park for a sail on the lake. Then they came home."

"Did she always do that? Tell you just what they did?"

"Why . . . no! Just the opposite. She never talked about what they did. But she told me all about it, even before she began to wonder what had happened to Alan."

"I have the uncomfortable suspicion," Blake mused, "that that ought to mean something."

Kathy's lip was curled in under her teeth, her eyes wide and distant. "It is strange," she whispered. "I never ask Jane what she and Alan do. And she's never gone out of her way to tell me . . . until last night."

Blake dropped his cigarette in the tray and stood up. "How are you," he asked, "on stumbling into dark rooms by mistake, finding clues, keeping up a hilarious line of chatter while guns press into your back, and so forth?"

"Would you repeat that please . . . slowly?"

"We're going sleuthing. I'm wondering if you're the correct, standard type."

"Sorry."

"That's two of us, but I'd like to find out who saw Alan last, besides Jane. We'll work backward and finish off with some of Pasquale's pastries."

Kathy looked up sharply. "How did you know about Pasquale's pastries?"

Blake grinned slowly. "Angel, not yet. We begin in the basement . . . and not on each other; it ain't ethical."

Kathy laughed and went into the bedroom for her coat. She stood in the dark room wondering what tenuous thing it was that made her doubt that she really knew what had brought Blake here. She felt so much at ease with him. There was an earthy candor about him that could not be anything but genuine. And yet she knew that she had changed her mind. She had thought to tell Blake about the ticket, to ask what to do about it. She wasn't sure now.

Pete was backing a custom-built car onto the lube hoist when they came down the stairs into the basement. He stepped out of the car, and Kathy said, "Hello, Pete. Have you met Mr. Blake? He's a new tenant."

Pete said, "How are you?" and "Excuse me for not shaking hands." Then he glanced at Kathy and said, "Heard anything from your brother, Miss Palmer?"

"Nothing yet."

"He'll turn up."

Kathy glanced at Blake, who looked away at the long line of cars. "Did you see them," she went on, "when they drove in last night?"

"Sure. Don't you remember calling me?"

"Yes. Did Alan seem upset or anything like that?"

"I didn't talk to him."

"Oh. But you did see him."

"W-e-e-e-ll. Yeah, I saw him."

Kathy nodded slowly, then turned to Blake and took his arm. "Thanks, Pete. Good night." She gave a tug at Blake's arm, but he didn't move.

He looked at Pete and asked, "Did you see his face?"

Pete looked Don Blake over slowly with neutral gray eyes. "No," he said, "I didn't see his face. Just a sleeve. And he didn't say a word."

"Did you notice that at the time?"

"No. I didn't think about it until I heard he was missing."

"Have the police been around?"

"One guy. I told him they both drove in around ten o'clock. He just asked me when they came in."

"I wouldn't want Mrs. Palmer to get the idea her sister-in-law was asking unflattering questions. They were my idea."

Pete put the handkerchief away and said, "Who's been askin' questions?"

Blake grinned. "Some car you're working on there."

"Yeah. That's quite a hot rod."

"Seeing you."

"Good luck. . . . You, too, Miss Palmer. Good luck."

PART FIVE

A SOMATIC blonde with blooming red cheeks was behind the counter, and the juke box was giving someone a loud nickel's worth. The girl was drying a glass that would never be any dryer and staring off across the lake.

Kathy said, "Sounds like Duke Ellington."

The girl behind the counter grimaced, put down the glass and said, "That's the Herman herd, honey. What can I get you?"

They ordered root beers, and when they finished them, Blake took a picture from his pocket and showed it to the girl. He said, "Do you remember when you saw this man last?"

The girl took the picture and looked at it carefully. "He go with a real slick blond girl?" Blake nodded. "M'm. I think they were in here last night."

"Can you remember the time, approximately?"

"Lordy, no. What are they, crooks?"

"No, they're missing. We're trying to find out who saw them last."

"Oh. Gosh, that's too bad. They were awful nice people. They had something here at the counter and went boating, but I can't say what time it was."

"Did you see them leave?"

"No-o. I don't think so. We get pretty busy around here sometimes."

Blake thanked her and the girl said she hoped those people turned up, they were super. He slipped the picture back into his pocket casually and they went out and down the stairs to the pier. Kathy tried to keep the chill that spread over her from becoming an outward shudder. She had caught a brief glance at the picture, and Alan had not seemed to be in uniform. And why hadn't Blake offered to show it to her?

"May I see the picture?"

"Of course." He held it out to her with a puzzled smile.

She took it and studied it for a long while. She had never seen the picture before, but it was a recent one, and he was not in uniform. She gave it back to Blake and looked out at the lights moving along the boulevard.

"I went by the bank after I talked to you this afternoon," Blake said quietly. "They gave it to me. They also told me they were pretty sure Al's books would check with his cash . . . or hasn't that worried you?"

Kathy looked up and tried to say something, and her voice choked to a stop. She said it with her eyes and with the first full warm smile she had been able to muster since Alan had gone.

"I'll do the apologizing," Blake said. "I should have told you about it, but I didn't think you'd like my checking up on your brother."

"I—I'm glad you did."

A boy in a basque shirt and a leather jacket was handling the boats. It was a cold night, with a hovering blanket of gray cloud and a soft keening wind. But there were people in the boats, and it was several minutes before Blake got the boy aside. He showed the picture and asked if he remembered seeing the man before.

"Sure. Him and his girl been down here two or three times lately. You a cop?"

"Do I look like one?"

"I never saw one that did."

"I'm a friend of his. He disappeared last night. I'm just playing detective."

"Is it fun?"

"Up till now," Blake grinned. "When was the last time they were in?"

"Last night, I think. Yeah, last night. I haven't spent the buck she gimme yet."

"What was that for?"

"She prob'ly liked my build." He winked at Kathy. "No, I give 'em one of the big jobs."

"The big jobs?"

"Big boats, built to carry four. She wanted it, and they give me a buck tip a couple nights before, so I give it to 'em."

"Who paid you when they brought the boat in?"

"They don't pay me. Over at the box there."

"Remember who paid?"

"Yeah. She did. She gimme this buck tip as soon as she got out, then went over and paid."

"And the man?"

"Huh?"

"What did he do?"

"Went on up the stairs, I guess."

"Didn't you see him?"

"Sure I seen him."

"Talk to him?"

"Yeah, quite a bit. He was a nice guy. We talked flying. I'm getting my pilot's license."

"You talked after they brought the boat in?"

"Huh? Say, I gotta get back." He turned and ran

over to the edge of the dock and guided a boat in to the landing. The boat emptied and filled and started away again.

Kathy said, "We know they were here. What—what are you getting at?" She had made an uneasy guess at what was on Don Blake's mind, but it didn't make sense. You couldn't take someone out there and drown him. She felt the cold sharpness of the water and wondered with a sick horror at the things buried in the muddy depths of it. It was a crazy thought. Alan wasn't out there. He was warm and alive and well.

Blake shook his head and murmured, "I don't know what I'm getting at. I'm just poking around. This lake has to mean something, though."

"But why?"

"Because it doesn't ring true. They say the two of them have come down here two or three times just lately. I don't know your sister-in-law, but I've met her and I've talked with her. And there's something strictly out of character about Mrs. Palmer sailing around in a smooch boat on this poor man's Lake Tahoe. So maybe it means something."

Kathy fell silent, her eyes pulled back unwillingly to the water, and she tried to see the boats on it. She found that she couldn't. Beyond the rim of light from the pavilion the lake was a great dark shadow. The boy came back over to them and Blake put a dollar bill into his pocket and said, "Thanks for the help. You said you didn't talk to the man after they got through boating. That's right, isn't it?"

The boy took the bill from his pocket, looked at it and put it in the side pocket of his gabardine slacks. "I don't think so. I think he just said good night or something and went on up the stairs."

Blake grinned. "You're not really sure of that, are you?"

He looked up at Blake then with a slow frown, and said, "Say, maybe you'd better talk to Mr. Hoxey. He's the boss."

"Why? That seems like a simple question."

"It sounds kind of hairy to me. I'd lay odds the blonde ain't missing. Right?"

"This is just between us. I'm not the law. Did he say anything to you when he got out of the boat?"

"I think he did. I was right there when he got out."

"See his face?"

"Yeah."

"How many hours do you have toward that license?"

"Sixteen. And do I love it!"

"Stick with it. I think the airplane's here to stay."

They both grinned, and Blake went on standing and saying nothing. And after a while the boy reddened slightly and said, "Okay, so I didn't grab his arm and do a slow take, no. But forget it, chum." The grin was weak now. "Nobody would pull anything as corny as that."

"I guess you're right. There's a boat docking."

They said very little driving back to the Chateau Michel. They rolled down the cold gray ramp and along the double row of cars to the place at the far end that had been assigned to Blake. It was dark there when he cut the lights, and Kathy felt suddenly tired. She made no move to open the door.

She told herself that she didn't want to go upstairs and close her door behind her and go to bed with the loneliness and the gray and formless thoughts that waited for her there.

"We'd better say good night here," Blake said. "Things will be easier if we aren't seen together too much right now."

"All right." she whispered, wondering what he meant by "say good night." She would wait and see. They were quiet for a while, and Blake smiled suddenly and said, "I made that sound like quite a project—saying good night—didn't I?"

"I thought so."

From somewhere near the ramp, a motor roared and the echoes gathered and resounded and died away. And Kathy was still waiting.

"Ten days in town," Blake said. "I don't think you'd go for that kind of a deal, would you?"

Kathy smiled. "I probably would. But I see what you mean."

She thought Blake flushed a little when she said that, but he studied her with a kind of puzzled assurance, then leaned forward and kissed her softly, lightly, on the mouth and said, "You haven't anything to worry about, Kathy. But be careful after you get upstairs, will you?"

'You're very helpful, Donald. With one hand you give me something to shoo the blues, and with the other you take it away. I'm afraid you'll have to give it back."

"Who's this guy Donald?"

"After that kiss, 'Mr. Blake' would seem a trifle stilted. But I don't think it quite called for 'Don.' "

"Your attitude's a little too wholesome, angel. It

disturbs me. I'm thirty-one, and the women I grew up with come equipped with a full set of coy guilt complexes."

"Would you like me to develop some? They sound like fun."

"Never mind. And don't get the idea I'm bashful," he grinned. "As a usual thing, I have all the subtlety and suave assurance of a rock crusher. It's just that when I kissed you then I saw a pair of carpet slippers as clear as day."

"How charming! And did a neon light flash on and off with the words: 'From this day forward'?"

"No, the words were: 'This is it, chum. Think fast.' "

Kathy stopped smiling quite suddenly.

"Don?"

"Yes."

"I—I don't think I get it."

"I don't want you to, baby. We . . . have a few bad days ahead of us, I'm afraid. In the morning you should go by police headquarters—"

"All right. Shall I go upstairs first?"

"Yes."

Kathy got out of the car and closed the door. She said good night. Blake was lighting a cigarette, and he nodded and Kathy walked away.

THE morning sun was warm, and it lay heavily on the still air of the room. Jane was asleep. She had searched the apartment for the ticket until she had fallen, fully clothed, on the bed, exhausted. And now she was dreaming. She was standing in a magnificent room and people were coming through a great arched door in evening dress. They came in one by one and shook Jane's hand and walked on. They were all women, and although neither they nor Jane seemed to notice it, they were all about twice Jane's height. Jane would look up at them and smile faintly, and they would touch her hand distantly and walk on. And somehow she would never quite hear their names.

She woke suddenly and sat. up. "Sharber," she whispered. "That was his name. Sharber." She looked at her watch. Nine-thirty. She ran into the living room to the phone and dialed information and asked if there was a number listed for a service station on West Adams owned by a man named Sharber. There was. Jane called the number and a heavy voice answered.

"Mr. Sharber?"

"Yes?"

She told him who she was and that Alan was missing, and Mr. Sharber said that was bad.

"Mr. Sharber, you were at Ipswich in England, weren't you?"

"For the duration. Longer than Al was, even."

"Did you ever know a pilot named Don Blake? A friend of Alan's."

"Don Blake? Was he at Ipswich?"

"He says he was."

"I sure didn't know him. Of course, a lot of good men went through there. But if he came out alive I ought to—"

"Mr. Sharber, can you come up here this evening?"

"Where?"

"To my apartment."

"Wh—"

"I want you to meet this man. You would know in five minutes if he isn't telling the truth."

"Sure, Mrs. Palmer. I'll be there. What time and how do I go?"

Jane answered his questions and hung up and stood motionless at the phone for a long while.

She was washing shaving cream from her fingers. She had finished the search. And now, desperately, she was going about the house looking into things she had missed the first time. She had just pushed her hand down into Alan's jar of shaving cream to find nothing there, as there had been nothing everywhere else she had looked. There were things he kept at the bank—an extra coat, a humidor, some books.

Jane brightened. The humidor. Full of tobacco, it would make a fine place to hide it. Or in one of the books. It was all right. She would find the ticket. And there were other things to think of now. There was Kathy. And Don Blake.

At three-thirty someone tried to open the door. The knob rattled and a knock sounded sharply, but not loudly. Jane opened the door and let Danny in. Danny looked bad.

Jane said, "Did you get it?"

"The best, duchess. Nothing but the best for you, duchess," he said thickly. "I say let's kill these people in style." He reached into his pocket and brought out a small brown bottle. It was almost full of a white polished powder. "Cyanide," he announced. "The poison preferred by nine out of ten suicides! Ask your doctor."

Jane took the bottle from him and held it tightly. "How do I use it?"

Danny bleared up at her and said, "The best way is to get them to write a note saying they are tired of it all, and then have them agree to spike their coffee with it while you're visiting the bird farm at Catalina."

"How much do I use, Danny? Or would you rather we'd take it ourselves?"

Danny was a long time answering. Finally he said, "If you have to spike something while it's in a bottle, that's bad, the man tells me. Yeah, we got a bargain. He not only sold it to me, he told me how to kill people without getting caught. He says, 'Don't spike a bottle if you can help it.' That way the cops know it ain't suicide, see? You've got enough there to spike a whole pint, though, and they don't have to drink much of it to get a nice result." He stood up. "Let me hold that little bottle for a minute, tiger, while you go fix me a drink. All this talk has made me thirsty. And I like it neat, sweet."

Jane brought him some whisky in a wineglass, and some water. She gave him the two glasses and he drank the whisky down and ignored the chaser, and leered up at Jane through eyes that were watery now, and bright.

He said, "You know what that guy says to me after we finish our business? He says, 'Say, you don't look like the type of guy I'm used to dealing with. What d'you want this stuff for?' And I says, 'You mean you don't think I look like a killer?' And he says, 'No, I don't.' And I ups and pulls out my gun, see?" Danny jumped up and pulled a sawed-off, ancient Browning from his pocket and pointed it at Jane. "And I says, 'Why, man, I'd as soon kill you as spit.' And he backs up and turns six shades of blue-green, and says, 'Okay, I didn't mean anything by it, brother. You're a killer. I can see that now. You're a real killer.' " Danny laughed flatly and without mirth, and Jane stood cold and terrified, clutching the bottle of cyanide in her hand and letting Danny's laughter slap at her like a vicious hand. He stopped laughing suddenly and said, wonderingly, "I wonder what he'd of said if you had bought the stuff?" Then he put his gun away and left without asking if Jane had found the ticket.

THE table was set for two. No one was having dinner with Kathy. She was eating alone, as usual, but she didn't like to look at a table set for one. There was something about it that offended her, like a picture hanging at an angle. So Kathy always set the table for two, except at breakfast, when she just didn't have the time. The chop was lying on its stiff paper on the drainboard and she was taking the dish of peas and the milk carton from the refrigerator. She poured milk into one of the glasses on the table, and the carton was empty before the glass was quite full. That puzzled her. She had had only one glassful at breakfast, so there should have been more than two left. She opened the refrigerator again to see if the milk had leaked. The refrigerator was bright and dry and clean. She shook her head and threw the carton into the box under the sink. She put the chop into the skillet and turned the heat to medium. She was slicing a tomato onto her plate, and over the sound of the frying meat she heard the phone. She turned the electricity off and ran in. She stopped at the phone for a moment and waited, then picked it up.

It was Don Blake. He said, "Had dinner yet?"

"No, I haven't."

"You probably don't like to make your engagements this far in advance, but how about having dinner with me?"

"Where?"

"That sounds like looking the gift horse in the mouth."

"I just wondered what to wear, that's all."

"Oh. Well, I've been eating at Larson's. You can probably come just as you are. How are you?"

"Fine, thanks. I think I can find us a little better place to eat than that. Okay?"

"I was hoping you'd say that. I don't want to come up on the seventh floor. How about meeting me in front in—"

"Twenty minutes."

Kathy hurried in and undressed, put her hair up in a rubber cap and stepped into the shower. Twenty minutes later she was dressed and applying the last touches of make-up and feeling only slightly as if she had worked eight hours that day and had had nothing to eat but two doughnuts and coffee since breakfast. She studied herself critically in the full-length mirror on the bathroom door, and finally let herself admit that she was happy with the way the dress heightened the warm apricot color of her skin. She looked eighteen again. Maybe that was what was bothering Mr. Blake. Maybe she ought to tell him she was twenty-three last December. Then again— She suddenly realized she was hungry. She really ought to drink that milk. It would probably go sour if she didn't.

A large fly was hovering over the glass and Kathy waved her hand at him and he rose resentfully and settled on the light over the range. She picked up the glass. The phone rang. She hesitated a moment, opened the refrigerator door and put the milk inside. It was Blake on the phone, reminding her that in one minute she would be ten minutes late. "Be right down." She ran into the bathroom and took the claim check from the jar of bath salts and ran back to the door and pulled it open. She started out and stopped short, almost stumbling into Jane Palmer. Something dropped from Jane's hand and glinted brightly for a moment. Jane leaned down and scooped it up.

She said, "My. I was about to knock. I—I wondered if you'd have dinner with me."

"Thanks, but I can't. Got to run; I'm late." Kathy hurried to the elevator and stood there, white and trembling. Jane hadn't intended to ask her for dinner. Kathy knew that. And the thing she had knocked from Jane's hand was a key. But Jane must have known she was home! It made no sense. The elevator settled to a stop and Kathy opened the door and stepped inside.

She found Don Blake in the great, dust-hoarding sitting room that nobody ever used. He was lighting a cigarette from the butt end of one he had just finished, and he didn't smile when he looked up and saw her. He came over to her and they started out.

He said, "Cigarette?"

Kathy shook her head and said, "You're supposed to tell me you don't like my being late, but

I'm worth it."

"I don't mind your being late. And you're worth it."

Kathy thought that over. They were outside in the evening dark now, and they walked up to Farrel, where his car was parked under a magnolia tree.

They drove up to Franklin, and Kathy said, "Excuse me, but was that a nasty remark?"

Blake laughed. "Sure." He turned left and got into the right lane. He was driving slowly and looking in the rearview mirror.

"Don't you think I'm beautiful?"

"Sure." He turned right, up a dark oak-bordered street that led nowhere. At the end of the block he turned left into an even darker and narrower street.

Kathy said, "Why don't we eat first and find a dark street after?" She was looking up at him with a puzzled frown, and half smiling at the same time.

"We've had company ever since we left the hotel. I was just making sure. I'm going to turn at the corner where that hedge is and pull up. See if you know the car as it goes by." He picked up speed, made a tight, hard turn at the next intersection, cut his lights and rolled alongside the dark curb. Seconds later, a dark sedan took the corner on two wheels, skidded, seemed to hesitate, then tore on up the street in hot pursuit of nothing at all.

"Know it?"

"No. But . . . wasn't it a woman at the wheel?"

"I couldn't be sure."

"I'd swear it was! And I'd swear it was Jane!"

"Why?"

"She's . . . I know it sounds crazy, but she's watching me! When I came out of my apartment tonight—just before I came down to meet you—she was just standing there in front of my door. And she had a key in her hand. I—I think a key to my apartment."

Don Blake didn't say anything, and Kathy knew he was waiting for her to explain why she thought it was a key to her apartment.

"We roomed together while Alan was overseas—right where I am now. As far as I know, she never bothered to turn in her key." Her voice was tight, the words thin and sharp.

"Relax, angel. She knew you were home, didn't she?"

"Yes," she breathed, "that's what makes it so—" The sentence trailed off and she reached into her purse and brought out the claim check and showed it to Blake. "She may have been after this. I found it in Alan's drawer yesterday."

Blake took it from her and held it down to the dash light. "What makes you think this is important?"

"It was hidden. Where Alan kept his gun."

"I'd like to check on this tonight. May I keep it?"

Kathy caught her breath and held it. The street had a distant silence as if the great city a few blocks away were a fiction. The echo of Blake's words hung quietly. They had seemed such casual words, but they had been strained through an ill-concealed excitement, and Kathy experienced again the sudden doubt that she had felt the night before when she had seen the picture of Alan. But Blake had explained the picture. Perhaps— And abruptly the curtain fell away from the thing she had known since yesterday: that Blake had not explained the picture at all! She had been with him until almost five o'clock. He could not have gone by the bank as he had claimed. There'd have been no one there.

"That . . . car has upset me. I'd like to go back home."

There was a hard silence, and then movement. She looked up quickly, and he was turning the key and the switch for the lights. He glanced down at her and said, "I'm on your side, angel. Remember that, will you?"

"I'll do my best."

"Would it be all right if I stopped by the drive-in for a hamburger?"

She nodded almost imperceptibly. He had dropped the claim check into a pocket.

At the drive-in, Blake asked her if she had gone down to see the police, and Kathy said that she had.

"Do you think it helped?"

"No. They hinted that Alan had left Jane for another woman."

"Anything else?"

"A man was seen leaving the car in San Diego. They said it was Alan, and that if I wanted to find him, I should try Mexico."

"That was right thoughtful."

"Yes. They told me not to worry. He'd get tired of her and come back home in a month or two. They said they all do."

"Do you think there's anything in it?" The strained undertone of excitement sounded again.

"No," she said. "There's nothing in it."

When they walked into the lobby twenty minutes later, there was a message waiting for Blake. Jane Palmer wanted to see him at his earliest convenience.

He said, "Let's go on up."

Kathy stepped into the elevator with him, but shook her head. "I don't think I should go."

"We're in the final stretch, angel. I think we'll know where we stand in a few minutes."

Kathy threw him a puzzled glance. "In that case," she said slowly, "I'd like to be there."

Jane was smiling when she opened the door, her face lightly flushed and her eyes bright. She was wearing blue satin hostess pajamas that Kathy had never seen her wear before, and when she looked past Blake into Kathy's eyes, there was only a fleeting hint of chagrin. Her "Come in" included them both. A tall man in a dark suit and an even darker scowl stood up as they came into the living room. Jane walked around them and stood beside the man and smiled at Blake with an air of repressed triumph, like a hostess about to introduce a minor celebrity to her friends from the suburbs. But. she didn't introduce anyone. She stood and watched them and let the awkward silence grow.

Then she drawled, "Mr. Blake, you and Mr. Sharber don't seem to know each other."

"Give us time," Blake smiled. "Maybe he's shy."

Jane laughed, and she let the laugh run through her words, "But Mr. Sharber was at Ipswich. You know, where my husband was stationed. Strange you don't remember him."

"Oh, that," Blake said mildly. "Don't give it a

thought."

The tall man said, "You never flew at Ipswich, Jack. What are you trying to put over?"

Kathy waited, her breath caught tightly in her throat. But Blake said nothing to the man. He grinned at Jane and said, "I still worry you, Mrs. Palmer. I can understand why—now."

"My husband is missing, Mr. Blake, and here you are, posing as his friend. Can you tell me why I shouldn't call the police?"

"Not offhand."

Jane frowned and shrugged her beautiful shoulders and said, "But who are you? What are you up to?"

Blake said nothing, the grin still faint on his lips; and Kathy knew, with a quick and empty sense of defeat, why she had believed in him. It wasn't that Blake had made it easy for her. He hadn't. But he had made it possible for her to live with the horror of knowing that something had happened to Alan. He had made it possible for her to fight Jane, and to pretend that she was not utterly alone. She leaned against the chesterfield and closed her eyes. A cold tension centered somewhere above her stomach and pulled at her throat. She thought of the ticket. Blake had come here for the ticket.

Jane said sharply, "Where is my husband, Mr. Blake?"

Kathy opened her eyes. Blake was shaking his head wonderingly at Jane. He glanced at the man in the dark suit and said, "We'll have to talk about it some other time, Mrs. Palmer . . . when you don't have company." He turned abruptly and started for the door.

The cold reached out and touched Kathy's heart and she cried out, "Don't let him go!"

Blake stopped and turned slowly, and his eyes met Kathy's. But they didn't tell her anything, and he said nothing.

Jane said, "Mr. Sharber, please don't let him leave!" She disappeared into the bedroom, and the two men studied each other casually. Sharber was young and as tall as Blake, and thicker.

"I'm going out," Blake said mildly. "I know you think you're doing the right thing, but you're on the wrong side, brother."

He moved toward the door, and Sharber stepped in front of him, but he did it slowly and with a worried frown on his face.

Jane's voice, sharp and cold, cut into the room, "Turn around, you."

Blake turned and looked at the automatic in Jane's hand. He grinned, but not heartily. He said, "A twenty-two. Won't make a hole big enough for the Old Floorer to get in even a finger." He backed toward the door. "Sharber, if you're a friend of Palmer's open that door for me."

The gun jumped in Jane's hand and the knuckles gleamed white. Blake stopped moving back. He wasn't grinning any more.

Jane purred, "That's much better. Now, Kathy, just why shouldn't we let him go?"

"Let her call the police," Blake cut in.

Kathy stood and searched Blake's face, and she thought she could see him shaking his head, no. The cold tension was sickening through her now and she wanted to run from the room, to run and keep running forever. She had never felt so terribly and irrevocably alone.

And then Jane's voice jabbed at her, "He's trying to gain time, Kathy! What's he done to Alan? What do you know about it? Quick!"

"Nothing! It isn't that. I—I found a ticket—" Her voice trailed off. The man was a fraud. He had lied to her every minute of the time since she had first run into him outside this door. But she knew that she had said too much.

The taut sharpness left Jane's face and she said quietly, in a tone threaded with excitement, "I'll take the ticket, Mr. Blake."

"Why don't we keep it legal?" Blake asked. "Call the police and I'll give it to them."

"I don't know why you should want the ticket. It covers a bag containing some things that mean something to me, but certainly nothing you should be interested in."

"Then there's no problem, is there?"

"Yes, there is. Calling the police would mean ugly publicity, made up out of nothing. So just give me the ticket."

Blake dropped his eyes to the gun. Jane's fingers were massaging the heavy grip with nervous impatience. He said, "Are you going to let me out that door, Sharber?"

Sharber was behind Blake. He moved up beside him now and said, "Why don't you give the lady the ticket, chum?" He sounded weary, as if he were anxious to get things settled, so he could get out of there.

"It's evidence."

"It's stolen property!" Jane countered. "If you try to leave here with it, I'm quite within my rights to shoot you."

The room was suddenly quite still. No one moved or spoke for a full minute; then, slowly, Blake reached into a pocket and brought out the ticket.

He turned it over and studied it, and Jane shrieked, "Knock it out of his hand!"

Blake grinned and tossed it to her. "Not necessary. I got it: four-one-o-eight-eight-six."

Jane's face flushed hotly, and for a brief and terrible moment Kathy waited for the gun to roar. But Jane knelt and picked up the ticket and read off a number. It wasn't the one Blake had repeated. Jane asked, "Did you get it?" and read it off again, different this time, and still wrong. Blake didn't seem to be listening.

Sharber suddenly rumbled, "Let me out of here!" and started for the door. Kathy jumped forward and squeezed past him as he opened the door. She heard him shut it behind him as she ran down the hall. At her door, she looked back. Sharber was striding toward the elevators, paying her no heed. Jane's door remained closed.

Kathy went into her apartment, turned the bolt and ran to the telephone.

Jane gave Don Blake an anthracite smile and said, "We seem to be alone."

"The gun still makes it seem crowded."

"I want to talk with you. But we can't do it here—one of them might be hysterical enough to call the police."

"You're not afraid of the police, are you, Mrs. Palmer?"

"They would be inconvenient right now. I don't

want you to get any false impressions, Mr. Blake. I wouldn't like to kill you. I've never killed anyone, and I don't want to now. But I'm desperate. My husband is gone and curious things are happening. I want to know what it is that he checked at Union Station."

Blake grinned. "I thought you said it was something of yours."

The icy smile dropped slowly away. "We can't talk here. I want you to walk down the stairs to your apartment. I'll be right behind you. If you do anything to startle me, I might get nervous and shoot you."

"And break that nice clean record."

"Let's go down, shall we?"

Again Blake's eyes dropped to the gun. Jane knew that he was questioning its authority, doubting that she would really use it. And she trembled and clamped her jaw to keep the trembling within her. She had found it hard to believe that pointing a gun at a man could do so much, that he could fail to see that little way inside her where the quavering fear and uncertainty lay. She lifted the gun and tightened the fingers that held the grip.

Blake's mouth turned up slightly and he said, "Okay, Mrs. Palmer. We'll go downstairs."

He waited while Jane opened the hall closet and felt for a coat and put it across her arm, so that it covered the gun. She followed him out the door and down the stairs to his apartment. They didn't meet any neighbors. He took a long time and made a good deal of noise getting his door unlocked. But they were inside now, and Jane was facing him.

She said, "Back up a little, please. You're too

close to me."

Blake grinned and backed up. "Shall I put up my hands?"

"Where do you keep your wallet?"

"On my hip, but you wouldn't want that—a couple of tens and a moth ball."

Jane wondered if he knew how right he was. She didn't want his wallet. She didn't care who he was. Things had got out of hand. The time had come for her to leave the bright island that was Southern California far behind her. And she needed only time enough to get to the station and to get the brown bag. If she could do that, everything would be all right.

"Turn around. I want to see who you are."

The grin faded slowly. He didn't move.

"Turn around!"

His eyes seemed to darken and the full mouth pulled down tightly. But she met his gaze and she hid her trembling. He turned and lifted his arm and looked at his watch.

"Take the wallet out and throw it behind you. And don't turn around until I've looked through it."

He brought his left hand around to his pocket and Jane filled her lungs and took hold of the gun by the barrel. She stepped forward and brought it around in a long swift sweep that broke heavily against the side of his head. He doubled over and turned and lunged toward her clumsily and fell on his hands and knees. He tried to draw himself up. Blood was running from a split across his ear. She brought the gun down again and felt the heavy jar of it along the barrel and up her arm, and Blake dropped on his face and lay very still.

The night was dark and moonless and without stars. The car waited for her quietly far down the street. Inside it, where she had put them earlier, were two traveling bags and a hatbox. Jane looked back at the Chateau Michel for a moment, then stepped in and drove downtown.

She went into the great arched station through a side door that led to an alcove given over to twenty-four-hour lockers. It was dark there, and from the far end she could see the people at the baggage stand and in the bright waiting room beyond. From the shadow of a pillar she watched. She had to be sure there was no one watching the place, and she wanted to go up when there were few people there, so that she would be there in the bright light a minimum of time. A large woman moved away with a small black bag in her hand, and Jane could see the first leather chair in the long row of chairs in the waiting room. There was a girl sitting there reading a paper. She was holding it up stiffly, and Jane thought she could see a part of her face in the shadow behind it. But Jane didn't have to see the face. She knew the dress and she knew Kathy's slender legs.

Blood pounded hotly in her throat and she moved back out of sight into deeper shadow. She wasn't afraid, not even angry. She was only indignant. It was so ghastly, so ridiculous, so wrong! That vapid, soft, sheeplike Katherine Palmer should be the one to fight her—and to win! Jane turned and went through the door and across the tiled patio into the cocktail lounge. The thought tormented her: had Kathy called the police? What would she have been able to say to them? Had she had time to call them?

The bar was long and narrow and dimly lit, and no one paid any attention to her. She walked almost to the end before she found what she was looking for. He was about twenty or twenty-two, with a round face, a thatch of red hair and an eager look in his eyes. His nose was thin and long, and it had recently hung over too many glasses of beer. He was alone at a table that was just large enough to hold two sets of elbows. Jane sat down across from him.

He seemed stunned slightly for a moment or two. Then he seemed to realize that this was it. This was the big moment the fellows all claimed had happened to them in Salt Lake City.

He smiled all on one side of his face and said, "I'm having beer. What do you like?"

Jane leaned forward and said, "I need a little help. How'd you like to do a lady a big favor and earn five dollars?"

The boy's smile clung to his face by sheer will. The soul had gone from it. "What kind of a favor?"

"I have to get my bag from the check stand. My . . . ex-boy friend is in there waiting for me to show up. I'd like you to get it for me." She winked ever so slightly and added, "If you want, I'll let you spend the five dollars on me."

The grin was well again now, and he said, "What are we waiting for?"

Jane watched him from the same pillar. Kathy was still there, still reading the same page. It was the boy's turn now, and he handed the ticket across the low metal counter and waited. Seconds later the brown bag was dropped before him, and Jane could hear the sound of it, and it was like heavenly music. The bald man behind the counter was saying something. The boy looked down at the bag, nodded his head, picked the bag up and took a few steps toward Jane. He changed his direction and walked over to a bench and put the bag on it. There was some yellow paper hanging on the bag. The boy unfolded this and looked at it. Then he picked the bag up hurriedly and walked toward her with a jerky stride.

He put the bag down in front of her and said, "Where's the fin?"

Jane decided he meant the five dollars, and gave it to him. He said, "Thanks, lady. I'll be going now." He hurried down to the end of the alcove and out the door.

Jane tore the yellow sheet from the bag and read it. She read it slowly twice. Then she wadded it into a tight ball and threw it against one of the lockers. She picked up the bag and walked out into the moonless night.

THERE was a rich and ringing quality about the darkness in Blake's room. It was a matter of sound and feeling rather than a mere absence of light. He groped his way up and his stomach rose with him and he fought it down and stood swaying gently. He tried to strike a match with a thumb that was like a French bun. He walked until he came to a wall and he scraped the match across it, and it sputtered and lit. He looked at his watch. The match burned his finger and he dropped it. Twenty-five minutes. It would take almost that long for her to drive down there. He felt his way around to the wall switch, turned on the light, and went into the bathroom to run cold water over his head.

Twenty minutes later he was walking through the great glass door that was the main entrance to the Union Passenger Station. There were ten or twelve people milling about the stand, none of them Jane Palmer. He walked on down toward the waiting room, telling himself it wouldn't do any harm—or any good—to sit down for a while. He noticed the newspaper first because it was obvious that someone was hiding behind it. Then he saw who it was, and sat down beside her.

Kathy lowered the paper slowly and the warm olive of her skin became warmer and darker, and she stared past the people at the edge of light and beyond them into the station's great dark vault.

"I—I half expected you to walk in here with Jane on your arm."

"She didn't like my company. I thought she made it painfully obvious."

The flush deepened. "I suppose you think I'm a special kind of menace." She didn't wait for Blake to answer, but hurried on, "What else could I do? You didn't explain. Everything you've ever told me was a lie." She stopped abruptly and turned her eyes toward him and added, "Wasn't it?"

"I'm afraid so, angel."

She looked away then, and after a while she said, "Where did you get that picture of Alan?"

"From his employer at the bank."

"You couldn't have. It was far too late."

"I'd already been to the bank, Kathy—before I

found you coming out of the apartment with a passkey in your hand. I heard about your brother at one o'clock. It was a five-line story in the midday edition of the News. The story mentioned where he worked, and I went by there to find out if he was in the clear."

"But why?"

"Because I wouldn't have been interested if he hadn't been."

"No, I mean why are you doing all this? Who—"

"We'll have a long, long time for explanations, angel. In the meantime, Janie goes her sanguine way."

"She hasn't been here yet."

"I'm afraid she has. Why didn't you call the police?"

"I did! As soon as I got to my apartment. They asked a million questions, and before they got there, I found you were both gone, so I rushed down here. I knew if I stopped to call the police again, she'd be here and gone before I finished spelling out answers."

"Would you by any chance remember that ticket number?" The tone was a quiet combination of chagrin and apology.

He made a fleeting grimace, and Kathy glanced at the split ear and saw the swelling above it and kept her silence. He stood up slowly, and Kathy rose with him and asked if he thought she should go home.

He nodded and said, "She had a friend—the man with the pipe wrench in his pocket. She probably had him pick it up."

Kathy took a quick breath and formed a silent,

"Oh." She whispered, "That's it. Everyone who came to the stand acted like everyone else. They took their baggage and walked away without giving it a second glance. But one man got a brown bag and took it over to that bench and looked at it as if he'd never seen it before. Then he took it around where those lockers are."

They were walking toward the big glass exit. At the alcove they stopped, and Blake nodded and said, "Doors leading out to the patio. Nice and dark all the way to the parking lot."

He put his hands in his pockets and tried to let the thought seep into his mind gradually, like a man stepping into a cold lake. She was gone. She had got what she was after, and there was nothing more he wanted to do about it now. From now on, it was strictly a police show. There was a taste of brass in his mouth.

Beside him, Kathy moved abruptly and stepped into the shadowed alcove. She was kneeling at the corner of one of the lockers. She came back out into the light, unfolding a sheet of yellow paper. She looked at it for a long while and held it out to Blake. Her eyes were dry and hot, her lips pulled flat against her teeth.

"I noticed some yellow paper," she said, "attached to that brown bag."

It was cheap scratch paper with a printed inscription: WRITE IT, DON'T SAY IT! Under this, someone had scrawled with grease pencil: "Guy who checked #410886 says to turn it over to police if it's claimed by a woman. In my book it says we give it to whoever has got the check. Right?" This was followed by an initialed instruction in neat red pencil: "Call me or Jameson if woman presents claim check #410886."

Blake folded it thoughtfully, and Kathy whispered, "It doesn't leave much to—to hang onto, does it?" He shook his head and dropped the paper into a pocket.

"You've got to tell me," Kathy said evenly, "what you have to do with all this."

"That's right, angel. We've got all the time in the world now."

Her eyes softened then, and she raised her hands and formed them into small hard fists. "I should have followed him!"

"Who?"

"The boy. The one who picked up the bag, but he looked so. . . harmless!"

"Why do you call him a boy?" Blake's voice was suddenly sharp.

"Why . . . he was. Twenty or so." And then, seeing Blake's sudden attention, she added, "He was tall, with red hair."

Blake reached out and took hold of her shoulders and pressed them. He seemed to have found a sudden new increment of energy. "Go home, angel. I'll call you later! I haven't anything but a license number and a vague memory of a man about thirty with plain brown hair. But I'm going up to the city hall now for some help."

CONCLUSION

IN the hard moonlight the row of court apartments looked like a motel on the edge of a ghost town. Jane pulled the brown bag from the car and hurried up the walk. A dim light shone behind Danny's door, and she rapped sharply, still holding tight to the torn handle of the bag. A quick movement sounded behind her and she turned sharply. A cat loped across the walk and disappeared into the dark. She rapped again.

The door opened slowly and Danny's face was there, pale, unshaven, a little sick about the eyes, the mustache looking like the patch of lawn under Jane's feet.

She pushed past him and said, "Lock the door, Danny. Pull the blinds."

He glanced at her dully and licked his lips. "Go away," he said thickly. "Creep back out."

Jane put the bag down in the center of the floor and smiled. It was a warm smile, reassuring, unaggressive. She said, "I found the ticket, Danny. It's all clear sailing now."

It was profoundly quiet in the room. The endless rhythm of the crickets' wings sounded all about them, and from across the way a laugh rose and broke crazily in midflight. Danny turned and bolted the door and pulled the blinds. He stepped toward the bag and looked down at it. He lifted it and dropped it on the bed, then turned suddenly, sharply. Jane stood quietly watching, and Danny's eyes were puzzled now. He stepped close and patted his hands against her pockets and along her sides, and opened her handbag.

Jane smiled when he finished, and said, "Disappointed?"

"Worried. I don't get it."

"We're going to Mexico tonight. A woman traveling alone would attract too much attention."

He grinned weakly. "That's better. For a minute you had me worried. Don't ever change, tiger. You're perfect in your way. I don't think I'd like you with a heart."

Jane looked hurt. "Open the bag, Danny. It's all ours!"

He turned slowly, and Jane stepped up beside him. He unbuckled the straps and knocked the clasp away and lifted the dusty top. The money lay as clean and pure and full of promise as Jane remembered it from that night so very long ago. Danny put his hands down through the packets until they rested on the bottom. He shook his head slowly and straightened up.

"Let's have a drink," he said huskily.

Jane put her hands on his arms and pushed him down onto the bed. She sat on the floor in front of him and said, "In a minute, Danny. First you've got to tell me about it. How much is there? And where did it come from? And can we use it safely?" The voice was soft, her face flushed and earnestly beautiful.

Danny looked down at her, absently at first, and then attentively, with eyes that were suddenly bright and dark.

"There should be forty grand, tiger. Forty thousand round simoleons. And I never thought I had it in me." He stopped abruptly, a closed-mouth grin across his face. "I'll get us a drink."

"Danny, wait. Someone threw that money into our car," she prodded. "It was meant for you. Who was it?"

Danny laughed. "You really do want to hear about it. I'm tempted to blow a brass trumpet, make like I'm one of the big talent. But I'm not. It was luck, old dumb Danny luck. I stumbled onto a racket, tiger. A guy with three floors of mahogany in the Union Building has this racket. He's a big insurance agent, and a politician on the side. He sells policies on things like bridges, aqueducts and stuff. Who ever heard of anything happening to a bridge, see? He figures he's as safe as a goldfish, so the policies don't ever go back to New York. They're just pieces of paper, and he pockets the premiums."

Jane sat up, interested. "But . . . how in the world did you ever stumble onto a thing like that?" She had almost emphasized the "you" and had caught it just in time.

"There's a club I belong to, off and on," Danny went on. "The county clink. I got friendly with a man who was in overnight for drunk driving. He had something eating him, and I got the idea it was worth a dollar or two. When I got out, I looked him up and bought him a few drinks. His name was Haskell and he was comptroller in this insurance company. He had a copper heart." Danny winked and said, "That's just the opposite of you, tiger. It took me less than three weeks to find out he was drinking 'cause he'd found out about the racket and couldn't make up his mind whether to be honest or bend a little. He bent. I was to be contact man. Two weeks later he drove his car into a lamppost." He snapped his fingers and leaned back against the wall. "Luck. Like hitting the Irish Sweepstakes. I sold my pigeon a bill of goods: I'd take one payoff and dust. He'd never hear from me again. He bought. And here we are. . . . Let's have that drink."

Danny got to his feet and reached down and helped Jane up. "All right," she said. "Make them stiff."

He went into the kitchen and came out again with two thick glasses and a quart bottle with about a pint of amber liquid in it. He poured each glass about a third full and handed one to Jane.

He grinned and said, "Eight hours ago I swore off this stuff. Well, tiger, here's to crime."

Jane nodded, her eyes empty and wide. She lifted her glass, and Danny raised his and drank it down. He lowered the glass slowly and thoughtfully. Jane's remained untouched in her hand. She held it out stiffly and her eyes were bright and full of incipient terror. Slowly, dull surprise and uncertain panic rose in Danny's face, and he dropped the glass and stared wildly. He moved and Jane backed against the wall, choking back a scream, holding it in her tortured throat. Danny took another step toward her and retched and pitched forward at her feet where she stood arched against the wall. He was curling up now like a leaf on a hot stove, jaw locked open, eyes staring and glazed, the pale skin turning a bluish gray.

It was a long time before Jane moved, slowly,

and stepped around him. She picked up the bottle and went into the kitchen and poured the whisky from the bottle and glass down the drain. She rinsed them both carefully and put the glass in the cupboard and the bottle under the sink. There were other bottles there, and she found one with some whisky still in the bottom and put it on the drain board. From a pocket she took the brown bottle that still held a few grains of cyanide, rubbed it between the palms of her hands and laid it beside the empty bottle of whisky.

SERGEANT LARSON was a large, pink man with orange hair, and eyes the color of skimmed milk. He sat in the back of the police car with Blake beside him and his partner at the wheel. He was thinking about the next police exam and wondering if he should bother to take it. The car was headed for some place on North Detroit. He wasn't too clear on why they were going there, but any excuse was good enough these days if it would get him out of the Homicide office, with its sticky layers of orange varnish and the commingled odors of vice and sanctity.

The car stopped for a red light, a lone man walked jerkily by, and Larson found himself wondering, haunted by a statistic. Was he one of them? Every year in L. A. twenty murders, more or less, slipped quietly into the limbo of the unsolved. So there was a large regiment of killers wandering loose in the city now, and although it didn't trouble Larson particularly, he found that he could never quite forget it.

On Beverly the driver used the red light and

touched the siren a few times just for fun. He was young, trap-mouthed, and Larson suspected him of reading books on police administration When they turned on Detroit the red light was off, the siren long silent, and a few blocks up they rolled quietly to the curb. Larson took the lead, walking with a tired, lumbering tread, yet quietly. Light was on inside the place he was looking for, and he rapped a couple of times before he tried the door. It opened under his hand and he went on in.

He stopped to look down at something hidden from Blake by the half-open door. The driver went on in, and Blake could see it now—an arm twisted grotesquely, two legs in the spent, flat significance of death. Larson rumbled, "Close the door," and his partner kicked it shut. Blake lit a cigarette, and after a while the crickets began a timid roundelay that swelled to a hectic chorus.

They stopped abruptly when Larson opened the door and said, "Come on in out of the cold."

Blake said, "Thanks. Noisy out here too."

Larson pointed to the bed and said, "Sit down. I'm not trying to scare you, but I'll stand." His partner was using a phone at the end of the room.

"I'm afraid I wasn't listening like I should of. Tell me again why you expected to find a woman out here and why I should've bothered coming out with you in the first place. I don't think you mentioned any bodies."

"I mentioned a body, but not that one. I hadn't expected her to kill him."

"She didn't."

"No?"

"And if you told me anything downtown that

proved her husband is dead, I think I missed it. Body in the morgue?"

"I think it's in McPhearson Park Lake."

He smiled down at Blake. "How'd she do that? The lake's surrounded by four of the busiest boulevards in town. Or are you telling me she hired a boat with her husband and brought it back alone?"

"More or less. Our friend on the floor was staked out on shore somewhere. She brought him back."

"Neat. How do you know all this?"

"I don't. But I think it's a hunch worth testing."

Larson shook his head and grinned. "Body'll come up in five days. Mind if we just wait?"

"If she put it there, she put it there to stay."

Larson thought about that for a while, hulking quietly and running a hand through his hair. "How many times you see her with this man?"

"I haven't seen the man."

"Take a look."

Blake stood up and leaned down to look at Danny's face for a brief moment. He sat down again and said, "Just once."

"Could you prove that?"

"No."

"Anyone else ever see them together?"

Blake frowned and waited awhile before he spoke. When he couldn't feel his pulse pounding in his throat any more, he said, "Help from private citizens is strictly *verboten*, is that it?"

Larson shook his head. "I think *you're* trying to get the help, brother. You asked us to put out a pickup on Mrs.—what was her name?—Palmer. I've seen these dodges before—private operators trying to get the department to do their leg work."

Blake said, "Maybe I'm naïve, but that looked like a corpse on the floor."

Larson turned to the trap-mouthed man at the end of the room and snapped, "Grimes, get ahold of whoever's working on that Palmer case. Let's get squared away here and now." Grimes went to work at the phone again, and Larson said, "There's only one thing that keeps me from writing this off as plain and simple suicide. You brought us out here, so maybe you know what you're talking about. If it's murder, I've never seen it done neater. The guy took poison, and he drank it from his glass. There isn't any in the bottle out there. . . .Why you so anxious to put the finger on Mrs. Palmer?"

Blake hesitated for a long moment. "I'm a friend," he said, "of her late husband's."

Grimes was talking with someone now in a low flat voice, and there were long intervals of listening.

Larson shot out, "Who you working for?"

"No one. I'm a boy scout."

"You're a guy with an angle. What's this Palmer woman got that you'd like to have?"

Grimes hung up and turned to Larson with a flat grin that carried an overtone of viciousness. He said, "Jim Breach had the case. It's the old story. Grass on the other side of the fence had more sex appeal."

"How about the lake?"

"The guy's sister made a report that got Jim a little worried, so he checked the lake. He says it's all clear there."

Larson turned to Blake and scowled as darkly as

his orange eyebrows and pink face would allow. "You'd better run along," he said. "We've got your address. Maybe you'll be hearing from us again."

Blake stood up. "You don't do anything about Mrs. Palmer?"

"Maybe. Depends on what we find here."

"She'll be out of the state by then."

"Sad. We'll send out one of our mounties."

Blake grinned slowly. "You know, I think you boys were an important part of Jane Palmer's plans. She'd had dealings with the law. I think she counted on a pattern just like this."

"Don't leave town. We may want some more of this charming chitchat."

Blake started toward the door and stopped, and when he spoke there was a note of faint hope in his voice, "Your department drags lakes every day. Can't you forget the way this all looks and drag McPhearson Lake? There's at least an even chance you'll find Alan Palmer down there somewhere."

"Sorry, Blake. The fire department does our fishing for us. We like to know just what we're doing before we put them to work. And McPhearson Park Lake is a big business. We wouldn't know where to look for the body, so we'd have to close the lake down for at least a day or two. You don't go into that kind of stuff half-cocked."

Blake nodded. He realized that from Larson's point of view he was a pretty slim breeze, and he was blowing no one any good.

"If I wanted to drag the lake myself, could I hope for some co-operation from your way?"

Larson looked puzzled then, and his tone was almost friendly, "About five years ago a guy thought his daughter was in that lake. He had to rent the lake and hire a crew. Before his daughter turned up in Merced, he'd spent four thousand bucks and had a lawsuit on his hands."

Blake nodded distantly and the taste of brass was bitter on his tongue again. He turned slowly and someone tapped gently on the door. Larson stepped past Blake and said, "That's the lab crew." He opened the door and a slender girl almost stumbled into the room with a paper bag in her hand. The bag dropped and split and four bottles of beer rolled out onto the bare carpet.

She stood shocked and immobile, staring in quick panic that slowly turned to anger and darkened her face. It was a square face with hard bone under it and eyes that were flecked with yellow.

"Who," she asked, "are you?"

"You live here?" Larson shot back.

The girl had begun to answer, and then had dropped her eyes. There was a high, sharp catching of breath and the pockets of flesh under the high bones of her cheeks deepened.

Blake stood stiff and cold. The girl stumbling into the room had brought something back: Kathy telling him of Jane's standing just outside her door with a key in her hand. He knew now what it meant. The sweat was swift and cold on his forehead, and he took conscious hold on himself. She was lying dead now on her kitchen floor, or she wasn't. There was nothing he could do about it now.

The girl said slowly, "How did it happen?"

"Cyanide," Larson said gently. "Quick and painless."

The girl's eyes widened slowly and tears covered over them and hung tremulously, but did not fall. She whispered helplessly, "Danny—Danny killed his self."

Larson was quietly casual, "Why do you say that?"

"He—he had his heart set on a big deal—thirty, forty grand. It didn't come off."

"That doesn't mean he killed himself, now does it?"

"He did it. I was with him when he bought the stuff. He wouldn't tell me what he was gettin'."

Larson moved abruptly and disappeared into the kitchen. He brought out the small brown bottle on a handkerchief and showed it to her. He said nothing at all.

The girl nodded distractedly. "Yes," she cried, "in that! White, like salt!"

Larson turned his head slowly toward Blake, and the muscles along his jaw pulled tight. "Friend, you can go now," he said thinly. "Sorry I'm not able to give you an oak-towel rubdown. But I'll be seeing you again. Real soon."

KATHY'S door was locked. Blake had taken a cab to the Château Michel and had tried to pace the floor of the five-by-five elevator as it ground slowly upward. Now the door was locked and no one was answering to the sound of his knuckles against the wood. He rapped once more, and again more loudly as the silence deepened. The stillness had taken on the quality of an unutterable answer. He went away from the door and found the manager's apartment, and the manager listened and watched

Blake's tight-lipped face and gave him a key without questioning.

The door opened into darkness. There was hope in that. He found a floor lamp and turned on light and the hope faded. The coat she had worn that night lay over the sofa. He walked slowly to the kitchen and put his thumb against the switch. The sterile whiteness of the room leaped at him. It was withdrawn, neutral and empty. He walked to the bedroom, hurrying now, and came out again a moment later with a wide and slightly idiotic grin across his face. He stood in the middle of the room for a moment and looked around, then walked to the door and opened it.

Kathy was there. Cold bright mist clung to her hair. Her eyes were dark and a little swollen, and a key was ready in her hand. She straightened slowly and said nothing. The peach-blow complexion grew suddenly warmer, and she walked inside and closed the door.

"Thanks," Blake said. "The least I expected was a bloodcurdling scream."

"I thought of it," she answered, and looked at him steadily out of starry, cold eyes. "What are you doing here?"

"Your sister-in-law seems to have had a supply of cyanide. I knocked first, but I didn't think that proved anything."

What he had said meant something to Kathy. Her eyes seemed to darken and she looked beyond him and whispered, "She tried . . . to poison me."

"How?"

"The milk. When I came home tonight I—I smelled it to see if it was still sweet."

"And it smelled like bitter almonds."

"It smelled strange. I never smelled a bitter almond.

"Come to think of it, neither have I. And now go ahead—tell me you threw it out and rinsed the glass." The tone was resigned, not bitter.

"Ye-es. I didn't know! Is it . . . important?"

"I think it was our last hope, angel. It means Jane got away with it. I suppose it was inevitable that she would. When you're up against Jane, you're faced with all the precision efficiency and built-in contempt of a slot machine." And then he repeated, almost to himself and with a small note of wonder, "She got away with it."

Kathy walked to the far side of the room. It was dark there and a window was open to the night. Blake knew what was coming. After a while she asked what he had to do with all this, and the tone seemed to say that in his answer she expected to find the last increment of iniquity on which her strength must break.

He went over to the window beside her and looked down into a dark garden below that he hadn't known was there. He didn't want to tell her what had brought him to the Château Michel for a while yet. But there was nothing now that would let him put it off.

He said, "There's one thing I'd like to settle first. I can't seem to remember what kind of carpet slippers they were that I saw last night."

"What kind do you like?" Her voice was flat.

Blake took her hands in his. Her hands were cold, and Blake's folded over them warmly and tightened, and Kathy looked up at him out of dark and steady and cool eyes and said nothing. He lifted her chin, and she shook her head then and whispered, “No.” Her lips were apart and her eyes questioned him, waiting. He leaned forward and kissed the warm corner of her mouth. She didn’t move and her lips remained open. He kissed the other corner and her mouth trembled ever so slightly and then closed, and her lips were warm and soft against his.

THE road was an endless slate, straight and smooth, with a chalk mark drawn down its middle, and high, wind-patterned dunes rolling away from it on either side with a kind of sterile majesty. The thrusting cold of the desert night had kept her wakeful and alert, but now the sun was reaching out over the hills with soft fingers, and her eyes were straining upward into darkness.

Yuma lay just over there where the sun was. Coffee and something to eat, and she would feel fine again. She could drive on to Nogales, where freedom waited for her. Nogales lay on the border, half in Sonora and half in Arizona. Jane knew only that, but that was enough. There it should be simple to cross over without too thorough an inspection, perhaps with none at all.

The rolling sand gave way to great flat stretches of mesquite and greasewood, with here and there a lonely palo-verde. She crossed the all-American Canal, brown and motionless, going nowhere; then, in the distance, the tall cottonwoods and clumped greenery that marked the Colorado. A few miles farther the road dipped and turned eastward, and before her stretched a long narrow building with an overhanging roof.

A man in a brown uniform signaled her to come in alongside. She slowed abruptly, trying to make it out. A sign on the building caught her eye and then blurred, but she had seen a word: INSPECTION. Panic and confusion swept over her and she drove her foot against the brake. A horn blasted behind her. A great Diesel truck was roaring down upon her. She threw the gear into second and the car rolled up to the building where the man in the uniform waited in puzzled irritation.

He had an umber, bloodless skin and opaque gray eyes. He leaned down and gave Jane a smile that was just a part of his job, like the drab and dusty uniform. He said, "I was scared that truck was going to stack you right up. Trucks don't have to stop, you know."

Jane pulled her lips back in an empty smile, her mind still caught in a quick-freeze of helplessness.

"I didn't know any cars had to stop," she said with a labored gaiety. "After all, isn't this still the U. S. A.?"

His set grimace softened and widened, and he said, "You bet it is. This here's only a fruit inspection. A quick look through your luggage and you're on your way." He turned the door handle. "All the bags right there in back?"

"Wait!" Jane gripped the sill of the door in desperate panic and tried to keep the terror out of her voice. "I—I don't want my bags looked at. I'm in a dreadful hurry. I've got to be in Phoenix. I—"

"Look, lady. You're wasting good time. How long does it take to open a bag, anyways?" He opened the door and Jane pushed him back and stumbled out of the car. She slammed it behind her and stood stiff and silent, and the man said, "What in— Say, what's the trouble, lady?"

She smiled brightly and put a hand on his arm gently. She said with soft confidence, "I've got a silly—but awfully important—reason for not wanting my bags opened."

"Sorry, miss."

Jane looked around. There were no other cars, and from an office at the end of the shed came a sound of typing. She made a playfully conspiratorial gesture and opened her purse. She took out a twenty-dollar bill and folded it so the denomination showed and held it between her fingers. "I swear," she whispered, "that I don't have any fruit in the car. May I go through?"

The man glanced down at the bill. "That could cost me my job."

"I can't afford any more; I'd have to let you look after all."

"You on the level? Absolutely no fruit?"

"I swear it!"

He looked casually in the direction of the office and palmed the folded bill. He opened the car door and Jane stepped in and closed it. He drawled, "According to the license, you're from L. A. Taking the long way to Phoenix, ain't you?"

Jane didn't answer. She started the car and roared away in an agony of grinding gears, up the hill and across the bridge, and down the gutted, dusty road into Yuma.

THE sun was behind her when she drove wearily into Tucson, but its gathered energy lay over the baked land like a thick, dry web. She pulled up onto the shaded island in the white glare of a filling station and put her head against the wheel for a moment and closed her eyes. She raised her head, and the attendant, a jowled man with matted hair, was walking from the shadowed recesses of a repair shed, wiping his hands on an oily rag. Jane told him to fill it up and asked, “How do I get to Nogales?” He told her in a few slow words and stepped to the pump. When he was finished and washing the grime from the windshield she said, “If you drive over into Mexico, do they take very long with the inspection?”

“Nope. They don’t inspect.”

“But I have bags in my car.”

“They don’t care.”

“But . . . what’s to prevent me from just driving right on down to Mexico City?”

“Nothing. Except there aren’t any roads.”

“Oh. You mean you couldn’t get to Mexico City from Nogales?”

“You couldn’t get anywhere from Nogales, ma’am. . . . That’ll he two-eighty.” When he brought the change, Jane said, “You can drive to Mexico City, can’t you? From somewhere?”

“From Laredo, Texas. That’s the only way I know of.”

“Laredo, Texas. How . . . far would that be?”

“Somewhere around a thousand miles. Want me to look it up?”

“No. No, thanks very much.”

So Jane bought a vacuum bottle and filled it with coffee and drove on. At twilight she pulled to the side of the road and stepped out. The ground slipped and righted itself, and she fell against the side of the car. She pushed back and breathed slowly, and in a little while she could straighten and stand. She reached into the front and took hold of the seat and pulled. The seat came forward and she wrestled it out of the car. Beneath the sheet-metal seat rest was all the space she would need. Now it contained oily rags, greasecaked bolts and a tire iron. She took them out and carefully wiped her hands. She stepped out to the center of the road and looked down its endless reach in both directions. She could see nothing coming. She hurried now, pulling the brown bag from the car, pulling the straps from it, tearing it open and stuffing the packages of money into the space under the seat rest until there were only a few packages left in the bag. These she threw on the floor in back; she would exchange them for Mexican money at the border.

She stiffened suddenly, bent in a grotesque gesture of hiding. A car was coming, the sound suddenly loud and near. She hurled the empty bag behind her, threw the oily rags over the packages that were visible, scrabbled in the sand and gravel for the bolts, and poured them over the rags. The car was applying its brakes now, pulling up behind her.

She picked up the tire iron and a voice said, "Havin' trouble?"

Jane turned slowly and looked back. A breeze had risen from the east and it played on her hot wet brow and cooled it, and for a moment she felt secure.

"I—I had to change a tire. All finished now."

The man was still in his car, just a round pale

blur of face and a bare arm. "Sure you're all right then? This is no place to get stuck."

"Fine, thanks. Thanks just the same." She laid the tire iron across the rags. It looked fine. She looked up and the man was getting out of the car. She could see a gleam of white teeth. He was a large man in a brown shirt and tight pants.

He was saying, "Guess the least a Texan can do is help you put that seat back in."

He was around at the open side of the car now, the seat lying on the ground between them. The smile was eager and friendly, and he looked at her for a moment, then reached down and picked up the seat. He lifted it through the door and dropped it onto the rest. He pushed it back and tried to settle it, but there was something wrong. It wasn't falling into place. He looked over his shoulder.

"You got too much stuff under there."

"No! It—it always sits that way. It's warped or something." Her voice had broken slightly and she pushed past him and slid over under the wheel. Her weight forced the seat back and it slipped and made a sharp little sound.

The man was grinning with frank amusement now. "Seems to be okay now, huh?"

Jane nodded helplessly. She was too exhausted to have to take this. She felt that she would be sick in a moment or that she would scream. This wasn't fair. This wasn't fair!

And then the man was whistling, an incredulous whistle, and he was reaching down and picking up one of the packages of fifty-dollar bills Jane had thrown on the floor in back. He looked at it a moment and raised his eyes slowly. Jane's head was cocked at an absurd and painful angle, and there was nothing she could do. She stared out at him in the thickening dark, realizing with a cool and distant clarity that this was no accident, but an affirmation of meaninglessness, the final idiocy, the ultimate violence.

The man was picking up the rest of the money. He said, "Now I know why you were so nervous. Quite a wad just to be kicking around!"

She didn't answer. And then she knew that she didn't have to. A car was coming toward them. She pulled on her lights. The man said casually, "Where do you want this?"

Jane took it and pushed it into her purse. She smiled and said, "It fell out of here when I took the seat out. Thank you for the help."

The approaching car was slowing now. The man stepped back and Jane started the car and drove off without shutting the door. It slammed shut and she pushed the accelerator to the floor and the car leaped forward with a bitter and complaining roar. The man behind her didn't try to follow.

It was daylight when she drove slowly into Laredo. It was like any other border town, hot, clinging low to the ground, a long street of money exchanges, tourist traps and shops where fly-harassed meat hung in the sun. Jane found the office of the Mexican consul.

A pale little girl with onyx eyes and blue-black hair sat at a desk and smiled up at her. Jane told her she wanted to drive to Mexico City to meet her husband. The girl wanted to know, in a polite way, how long she expected to stay. Jane said, "A few months," and the little girl asked more questions and made out a card. She took it into another room, came out in a few moments, handed it to Jane and said, "A pleasant trip."

Ina little clapboard office that looked like a Chinese lottery, Jane changed her money into larger-denomination pesos. She drove down the street and onto the bridge, paid her toll, and rolled across the dry river to where the Mexican customs officials waited for her.

There were two on duty, young, with eyes and hair like the girl in the consul's office, and with the same soft voices. But they were men, and Jane felt suddenly confident. One of them asked where she was going, and Jane showed him the card. He nodded and asked her to drive over to the right where her bags could be stamped. He didn't say "inspected," just "stamped." But they were inspected. Neatly, with a note of apology, and no further than what was visible. They did not even open the glove compartment. In a few moments it was over and they were saying, "You may pass," and "Happy journey," and Jane was driving on.

She was free. The sound of the car sang it to her; it echoed in the heavy beat of her heart; it danced in the bright miasma that hung before her eyes. She smiled slowly, and the car picked up speed and raced on down the long Pan American Highway.

THE desk clerk at Mexico City's Hotel Reforma had a smile that warmed, but never intruded, flattered yet remained impeccably impersonal. He gave Jane the smile, and nodded as she strode through the lobby. He watched her step into the elevator and thought about her after the doors had closed. When she had first arrived at the hotel, alone, he had come to a conclusion about her of which he was now frantically ashamed. But he had found no other answer to why one so very lovely should be so much alone, although he had pondered this enigma with a melancholy appetence for several weeks now.

Jane stepped out of the elevator into the hall. It was shadowed and cool and very much her own. She smiled to herself. She was infinitely happy. She felt her happiness as an energy and a force, as a triumph and a confirmation. She had discovered a terrible, sweet secret that only the courageous and the self-chosen knew: that the touchstone of value was in her own being and nowhere else. It had lifted her above the needs and fears of the faceless ruck; it had shown her a new dimension of freedom.

She was at her door now, and she stopped and brought out her key. She lowered the key and took hold of the knob. The door opened slowly under her hand, and an odor of burning tobacco came from the room. The shades were drawn against the bright sun and she stood irresolutely, seeing nothing, not moving.

A voice said, "Come on in, Mrs. Palmer . . . excuse me . . . Miss Petry, according to the register."

She stood where she was, trying to think, trying to place the voice. She had heard it before. She knew it well. But her mind had rolled into a tight suspension, and she could not move.

The voice came again, gently, "No one likes to walk into a dark room. Let's have some light."

There was a sound of movement, and light flooded the room, shining in a soft diffusion from behind the frosted-glass pilasters. He came toward her now and drew her into the room and closed the door. He walked with her to the ice-blue love seat and said, "Sit down, Jane. Nice place you have here. Nice furniture. What kind is it?" He sat down across from her and picked up his cigarette from a tray.

Jane smiled slowly, feeling only a mute irritation now at her own fright and fleeting helplessness. "It's bleached narra wood," she said. He blew a thin veil of smoke at the carpet. "It's a twist-weave carpet," she added. "Are you thinking of moving in?"

"After a fashion."

"Oh?"

"I'd like, say, half of the bonanza you brought down here with you."

"Bonanza, Mr. — What was your name? "

"It was Blake when you knew me. Yours was Palmer."

"And now we both have new names, is that it? I hope you didn't spend too much locating me—"

"It wasn't too difficult."

"—because I'm afraid I haven't any bonanzas . . . yet."

Blake grinned with stiff lips. "Forty or fifty grand, according to Danny's girl friend."

Jane's stomach pulled tight and a nerve began to jump visibly in her throat. The man was bluffing! He had never actually seen her with Danny. There was no connection between them and no way to make one! And she was suddenly without fear. The man was a criminal, and there was deep relief in that knowledge, and strength.

She rasped, "Get out! I don't know anyone named Danny and I haven't any money." Blake dropped the cigarette in the tray and looked at his watch. Jane repeated, "Get out! I swear I'll scream to wake the dead if you don't get out!"

Blake crossed his legs and said, "You're right, you don't have anything to worry about on Danny. You'll never go to the gas chamber for what you did to him. But you will for what you did to your husband. . . . I found his body."

Jane was a long time responding. She had had to work it out. If Alan's body had been found, it would be the police who would be after her, not Blake. She had been getting the Los Angeles papers. She'd have read of it.

The smile revived and warmed, and she said, "Where did you find him?"

"Right where you left him."

She gave a throaty laugh and said, "I shall begin to scream in just ten seconds. I have a loud scream. It carries."

She laughed again, and then Blake cut the laughter short, broke it abruptly, viciously, with a few cold words. "I let him," he said, "drop back in."

A pulsing, layered shadow closed over her mind, and for an endless moment she fought this fear with the even greater fear that she would betray herself. She heard herself whispering, "Drop . . . back . . . where?"

But even while she said it, she knew that he had won, and she began to find solace in it, and respite. She would pay him, and so she would bind him.

She would still be free. He had not answered. She rose and walked to the windows and pulled the blinds. The window was open and there was an odor of gardenia in the air. A few white clouds lazed low in the sky.

"How much," she asked quietly, "do you want?"

"I'm not greedy. I'll settle for half."

"That would be about fifteen thousand."

"I want twenty."

"There was only thirty."

"Twenty for mine. You're lucky I don't take it all."

She turned and walked back to the center of the room. "I don't have it here."

"Go and get it."

"You trust me?"

"Why not? You're more anxious to buy than I am to sell."

Jane nodded. "You'll wait here?"

"Uh-huh. You won't run away."

She walked to a closet and brought out a hatbox. "It's in twenties and fifties. The box is to carry it in." Blake nodded distantly and Jane went out. Walking down the flight of stairs from lobby to street, Jane told herself that she must not complicate things. She must go to the bank. The doorman called up, *"Coche?"* and Jane nodded. She was in the cab now, and she was repeating to herself that she must go to her bank and get the money and pay the man. There was a hard and lucid simplicity about it. They shared the money and thus they shared the guilt. But Jane found herself telling the driver to take her to another place. It was a shop she had seen many times, a sportsman's shop, a place to buy fishing tackle and riding equipment and guns.

The clerk was polite. The clerk agreed that the señorita might be wise to carry a small *pistola*. But before he could sell the señorita this, she must have a— He had difficulty finding the word and said, *"Permiso para portar armas."* He shrugged and shook his head.

In the cab, Jane shuddered, and once more felt warm relief. She was glad she could not buy the gun. The near folly of it appalled her, and she closed her eyes. She was driven to the bank, where she counted the money into the hatbox and returned to the hotel.

The room was dark again. She closed the door behind her and caught her breath. The lights came on and Blake was standing by the wall, holding a tiny automatic in his hand. He grinned. "Silly, my being suspicious of you, isn't it?"

Jane walked to the coffee table and dropped the box. "There it is," she breathed.

He dropped the gun into a pocket and came around the love seat to take Jane's purse and look into it. He took a quick glance at her trim figure and said, "No gun, Miss Petry? I feel almost slighted." He opened the box and began counting, using only the fifty-dollar packets. He counted it into two stacks, using only a small part of what was there. He looked up then and said, "It tempts me, but I guess that does it."

Jane frowned and asked slowly, "What's this all about?" Blake's attitude had taken on a subtle change, the face suddenly tired and without expression, as if he had lost taste for his victory. He sat down.

"I'm giving you," he whispered. "a strict accounting of your funds. You see, I needed some money, and I had to know for sure that Alan Palmer was in the lake."

Jane sank slowly to the love seat, feeling the muscles about her mouth begin to pull and stiffen. She waited for what was coming.

"I hadn't thought," he said quietly, "that I would feel any qualms. I had planned to enjoy this, to play cat to your mouse, to have a kind of sanguine bacchanal. But I'm not enjoying it. . . . You're going back, Mrs. Palmer."

Inside her now was a cascading chaos, a drawing sickness reaching through her and pulling with sharp, cold fingers at her throat. The feeling of having known Blake, of having known him long and well, lay heavily over her.

She breathed deeply and tried to make the words come out strong and cold, but her voice was a tiny thread of sound. "You can't take money and then—"

"The first stack is for a man named Montenegro. He has an army of detectives here in Mexico. That was why I let you go to the bank alone. The other stack is for a man named Hoxie. He owns McPhearson Park Lake."

Jane sat silent and bewildered, shaking her head as if she were denying something.

"I've got to have someone to watch you," he explained, "while Hoxie brings up Alan's body and I get our overworked constabulary moving. Montenegro has that job. You'll probably try to run away. I expect that, but you'll be wasting your time. Better stay here and enjoy the week you have left." He stood up then and pocketed the two stacks of money. He looked briefly at Jane once more and walked toward the door.

"Wait!" Jane shrilled, standing and almost stumbling after him. He turned and she stopped a few feet from him, feeling his unimpassioned contempt like a cold wave. "Please! Are—are you—"

"No, Mrs. Palmer. I'm not the law, if that's what you mean."

"Then—" But her mouth pulled spastically down away from her tongue, and what she had tried to say was gibberish. She stepped forward and took hold of his arms and shook her lovely golden head in frenzied agony until tears began to fall. And with the tears came release, and she cried, "Please! I'll give you the rest! There's almost forty thousand dollars! It's yours! All of it's—"

He took her hands away from his arms. His face was pale, immobile, blank. "You can't see it, Mrs. Palmer," he said, "but I'm riding a great white horse. These are boar-hide walls and I'm jousting with Evil."

Jane stared, trying to think of what he was saying, searching for hope or a promise in it. And then she saw the familiar thing in his eyes again, and she cried, "Who are you? Damn you, who are you?"

"Someone who couldn't let you get away with it, Jane. A killjoy."

Jane threw her hand out sharply, as if she were brushing something aside. What was he saying? What was he talking about? She whispered, "Why?" and her voice choked off and the tears came again. She repeated brokenly, "Why?"

Blake studied her with a distant detachment,

and over Jane's hopeless foreboding rose a faint anticipation of victory, and she smiled. She summoned all her flagging will and subtle artistry for that smile. She made it sweet and swift, and brave and pleading. And Blake's expression changed and he seemed to make up his mind about something.

He said coldly, "The name is Blanchard. Does it mean anything to you?"

Jane moved back slowly, the smile a wooden painted thing across her face. She put out a pink tongue tip to wet her lips, but they remained as they were, hot and dry.

"I once married a man," she croaked, "named Blanchard."

"Yes. And you also killed him," he replied.

He seemed suddenly to move, and Jane stumbled back. And then she knew he had not moved. The room had moved. It had become a bright hot void without dimension or perspective. She felt the hideous smile clinging relentlessly to her face.

He was talking again in a kind of monotone, "I was overseas when I heard of it. I knew he hadn't killed himself . . . even then. He was my father, and vanity wasn't one of his faults. He wouldn't have given a damn for failure."

Jane's eyes were just dead flesh now. She stared beyond him, beyond the wall, even beyond her fate. He turned and walked to the door, then looked back at her.

"Don't think," he said slowly, "that this was all a vendetta, Jane. Revenge is a tawdry spur. You inspire far more epic motives."

The words gathered inside her and echoed down the long bare corridor of her mind, round and hard and brittle, like the rapping of judgment. He opened the door, and she tried to move, but could not. He closed it quietly behind him without looking back, and left her standing and grinning emptily at nothing.

He walked down the cool, scented hall, and in the shadow there a little dark man nodded as he passed. In a far corner of the lobby Kathy waited with a pale, strained face. He found her there and smiled.

"It was a short honeymoon, angel," he said. "We're going home."

THE END

TO THE READER

If you enjoyed this book, you will be glad to know that there are many others just as well written, just as interesting, to be had in the Fiction House Press Library.

You will find the Fiction House Press Library online at

www.ingramcontent.com/pod-product-compliance
Lightning Source LLC
Chambersburg PA
CBHW060401030726
47497CB00003B/810

* 9 7 8 1 6 4 7 2 0 5 8 3 6 *